I0735212

ALL WE ARE

Haven's Bay Holiday Series

J.H. CROIX

This is a work of fiction. Names, characters, businesses, places, events and incidents are either the products of the author's imagination or used in a fictitious manner. Any resemblance to actual persons, living or dead, or actual events is purely coincidental.

Copyright © 2022 J.H. Croix

All rights reserved.

Cover design by Cormar Covers

No part of this book may be reproduced in any form or by any electronic or mechanical means, including information storage and retrieval systems, without written permission from the author, except for the use of brief quotations in a book review.

 Created with Vellum

" ... our first love is our last, and our last love our first." George John-Whyte Melville

Sign up for my newsletter for information on new releases & get a FREE copy of one of my books!

http://jhcroixauthor.com/subscribe/

Follow me!
jhcroix@jhcroix.com
https://amazon.com/author/jhcroix
https://www.bookbub.com/authors/j-h-croix
https://www.facebook.com/jhcroix
https://www.instagram.com/jhcroix/

Chapter One

THEA

"Great, just great," I muttered to myself.

It wasn't supposed to be snowing, but the weather was a fickle character in New England, specifically in coastal Maine. Although, I dare say, most anywhere in the world. The snow started out with light flakes floating from the sky. But as I continued my drive north, the snowfall began to get heavier and was coating the road.

Great timing on my part. I kept driving and managed just fine, although I was relieved to see the exit sign for Haven's Bay illuminated by my headlights through the thick snow. While I hadn't lived in Maine since high school, I lived in Boston and hadn't lost my touch with handling snowy roads.

But I was tired, and my nerves were frayed. My pride was also bruised, but I didn't even want to think about that. I was going to take some time off and stay at my childhood home and lick my wounds. Despite my cynical mood, a feeble cheer rose up inside me as I slowed to turn on to Main Street in Haven's Bay. My little hometown was picturesque in every season, and during the holiday season, it was straight off of a postcard.

The tall balsam tree anchoring the center of the town green had holiday lights glittering in the darkness. Lights were strung along the streets and storefronts, and the falling snow added a touch of magic to the scene. For the first time in days, my lungs filled completely when I took a deep breath, and the tension squeezing like an unpleasant band around my heart loosened. A few minutes later, I saw my family's mailbox and slowed to turn before slamming on my brakes. The lights were on, and two cars were parked at the end of the driveway.

"What the fuck?"

I had told my friend Jane she could stay for three weeks, but those three weeks were up. Her car was parked behind my brother Ian's SUV.

"Well, well, well."

Although they had just foiled my plans for a week alone, I kind of hoped maybe they would hook up. They both needed a little fun in their lives. My brother Ian was all work, work, work, and Jane shared that tendency. I adored her, but she was definitely on the serious side. If it hadn't been dark and snowy, I might've gloated a little.

I needed another plan before anybody noticed my vehicle at the end of the driveway. I backed up quickly and drove past my family's home, wondering if I could find a local hotel or bed & breakfast. About a mile down the road, I pulled into a viewing spot on the coastal road. My headlights arced over the snow, casting a glimmer on the dark ocean just beyond.

I pulled up my search app to see what I could find. It was a week before Christmas. I wasn't about to tell anybody in my family what was going on.

Me, the cynical one who'd sworn off relationships for years, had gone and proven myself right by foolishly falling for an asshole who'd completely ghosted me. I knew I could go to the house, but I didn't want to barge in and have to explain my unexpected appearance. If anything was happening with Ian and Jane, I didn't want to ruin it either.

Every local place listed showed as closed for the winter. Of course. Haven's Bay was a quiet, coastal town. While it was busy with tourists during the summer months, the winter months tended to be quiet with shoppers just passing through town.

"Well, I'll just go to the grocery store. Maybe somebody there can give me a suggestion," I murmured to myself.

The closest town with an actual hotel was a good forty-five minutes away. More driving in this weather definitely wasn't my preference. I tossed my phone into the console, adjusted the heat, and started driving again. The snow that had started to ease up changed its mind again, thickening heavily until the visibility was next to nothing.

I barely saw the dog that darted in front of my car, and when I slammed on the brake pedal, the brakes slipped and then caught before I swerved off the road. The dog dashed away into the darkness as my car rolled to a bouncing stop. The angle of my headlights told me everything I needed to know. I was thoroughly in a ditch. I thumped my head against the steering wheel in frustration.

Though I was physically fine, this was not good. Lifting my head, I glanced around with a sigh. I reached for my phone again, planning to call the emergency car service. Maybe I was being stubborn, but I really, *really* didn't feel like seeing anybody I knew tonight. Pointless though it may be, I wasn't going to call my brother and Jane for help. There was a reason I paid for the car service.

Only moments later, the friendly customer service representative assured me someone would be on their way within minutes. After I got off the call, I cranked the heat and leaned back in my seat. Maybe I could turn this into some kind of Zen experience where I just rolled with the punches. It was no big deal. Someone would tow my car out of the ditch.

My phone vibrated, and I lifted it to see a text alerting me that my driver would be here in five minutes.

"Hell, yeah," I murmured. "Fastest car service ever."

A mere three minutes later, I saw the headlights flickering in my rearview mirror, and the tow vehicle pulled over behind me. Another moment later, there was a light knock on my window, and I rolled it down.

"Hi—" One syllable was all I got out before whatever I'd meant to say next came to an abrupt stop.

Joe Martinelli was peering through the window. It only took a second before I saw the recognition dawn in his eyes. He looked startled for a moment before one corner of his mouth kicked up in a half-smile. My belly swooped as goose bumps prickled over the surface of my skin with the fiery shiver that chased through me.

"Joe," I finally managed.

"Hey, Thea."

"Are you the car service guy?" I could be the queen of the obvious sometimes.

"Course I am. My dad's garage has had the contract for, oh, probably since before I was born," he said with a shrug. "I run the garage now."

"You do?"

When he grinned again, my belly shimmied while butterflies fluttered about and my heartbeat kicked madly against my ribs. "At your service. Are you headed to your family's place?"

"Oh, no," I said quickly.

Joe looked a little confused. "Okay. Well, I'll get you out of the ditch, and you can be on your way then."

"Should I get out of the car?"

"That'd be best. You can sit in the passenger seat in my tow truck. It's warm in there. I won't make you wait in the snow."

"Okay," I squeaked. "Should I leave my car running?"

"Nope. Turn it off and put it in neutral for me."

I glanced around, eyeing the angle of the slope in front of me.

As if he could read my mind, Joe interjected, "It's stuck in a foot of snow in a ditch. Your car's not going anywhere. I promise."

"Right. Okay."

With alacrity, I rolled up the window, turned the car off and put it in neutral before grabbing my purse and climbing out. Like the gentlemen I knew him to be back in high school, he reached for me. He steadied me by the elbow as we walked through the snow. He even opened the door for me. After he made sure I was situated in the passenger seat, he walked around to the back of the tow truck.

This was not the first time I'd been inside a tow truck with Joe. Oh, wow. This wasn't just a walk down memory lane. It was a fast-forward speed drive. For a whole year, I'd had the worst crush on Joe in high school and barely contained my squeal when he asked me out. He wasn't the kind of guy I was supposed to have a crush on, at least according to my father. He was sexy, he was tough, and he carried himself with the edge of a bad boy.

But that wasn't all there was to Joe. It felt as if a fissure opened on the edge of my heart, an old scar torn open. I ached a little at seeing him all these years later. I'd really liked him, even loved him, and he'd been really good to me for the time that we'd snuck around and then officially dated. I'd had all of my firsts with Joe—first kiss and more.

I suppose he was my first heartbreak, except I broke his heart and mine in the process. All because my dad was an asshole. I felt tears stinging my eyes, and I closed them, taking a shaky breath and willing myself to get some kind of grip.

In the nick of time, I pulled it together. The blast of cold air that entered the truck cab when Joe opened it to climb in was enough for me to swallow through the thickness in my throat and blink my tears away.

"Give me just a sec, and we should have your car on the road. What happened anyway?" he asked.

"A dog darted in front of me. I slammed on my brakes and swerved. I missed the dog, so it's fine. Hopefully, my car is too. In any case, if there's a problem with my car, it was worth it."

Joe had been about to shift the gear on his truck, and his hand froze as he turned to look at me. In an instant, memories hovered in the air between us, shimmering like sparks.

"Of course, it was worth it," he said. "I think it might've been my dog."

"Really?!"

He cast me a rueful smile when he shrugged. "Probably. I live just down the road from here. He doesn't usually leave the yard, but somebody nearby has a dog in heat, and he keeps going down to their house."

I burst out laughing. "Oh, my god! That's hysterical, Joe," I finally managed when I stopped laughing. This time when I wiped the tears away, it was okay because he wouldn't know they were glimmering from a few minutes ago.

"He's home now. I got the call for this right before he showed up at the front door."

"What's his name?" I felt myself smiling. It seemed serendipitous that Joe's dog would've been the factor that set our paths to crossing again.

"Dexter."

"It might not have been him. I didn't get a good look at him."

"Well, I hope not," Joe offered with a wry chuckle. "If he was going fast enough for you to avoid him, that's a win." He glanced out the window as a car drove past. "All right, let's see what we can do here."

I waited while Joe turned the tow truck around and eased back slightly toward my car. He climbed out to do something with the tow cable before returning.

Once Joe got my car on the road, I hurried out of the truck. He had leaned over to check on one of my tires. When he straightened, he rested his hand on the hood. "You're not going anywhere tonight, sweetheart."

I ignored the achy twist of my heart at his endearment. "What? Why?"

"You have a bent tire rim. I'm guessing you caught it on a rock."

"Really?"

My belly was still spinning from the flip when he called me "sweetheart." I told myself it meant nothing, but my heart disagreed. He used to call me that back in high school.

As I stood there in the snow on the side of the road, all of these little annoyances that had nothing to do with Joe bounced into each other. Somehow, his presence and the old emotions attached to him brought everything rising swiftly to the surface. The rush of emotion toppled me right over the edge, and I took a shaky breath.

You're not going to cry. Do not cry. Not right now. You've got this.

I gulped in another breath, scrambling for purchase in the internal tumult while I felt as if I were about to crumple.

"Are you okay?" Joe asked.

My head whipped up. The second I looked into his eyes, I burst into tears.

Chapter Two

JOE

Thea Tate—my old high school girlfriend, the one who shined brightest in my memories and probably the only girl I'd ever loved —was crying on the side of the road in the snow.

Great. Fucking great. I'd never handled tears all that well, and my own emotions were feeling jagged tonight with this unexpected encounter.

"Hey," I said, pushing away from her car and stepping to her. "It's fine. I'll tow your car. We'll figure it out."

Before I could think it through, I was pulling her into my arms. The second she tucked her head against my neck, burrowing into me, it felt as if two lost puzzle pieces had been found and clicked together. My body felt electrified. The wind howled around us, and the snow blew sideways, striking in sharp spikes against my cheeks.

I slid my hand up and down Thea's back and forced myself to lift my head and step away, curling my hands on her shoulders. My heart felt scored and cracked open when she sniffled. "It's just a tire rim. I'll get it fixed as soon as I can," I assured her.

She nodded, knuckling at her cheeks to wipe her tears away. "I know you will. I'm not crying over that."

"No?"

She peered up at me again, blinking before her lips twisted in a wry smile. "It's just everything kind of piled up, if you know what I mean."

"Oh, I do." I felt the rise of her shoulders when she took a gulping breath. "Hop back in my truck because now I need to get your car on the flatbed."

She nodded. I walked her back and made sure she was situated in the passenger seat. It didn't take long before I got her car on the flatbed. My dad's old garage business made serious money these days. Back in the day, her dad thought I wasn't good enough for her. Now he was in jail, and my family had a lot more money than they did.

I didn't blame Thea for what happened, but then there was a splinter of frustration in my old anger. Her dad was the asshole, and jail was exactly where he deserved to be.

I watched as the flatbed rose slowly to level and checked the tie-down straps to make sure her car was secure. As I walked to the front of the truck, I leaned into the snow, which had picked up its pace even more.

A moment later, I glanced at her. "So, we're gonna go to my garage. I could take it to my house, but I don't want to leave your car out in the snow all night. If you're not staying at your family's home, where *are* you staying?"

Thea was quiet. When I glanced over, I saw that she was twisting her fingers together, a sure sign that she was nervous. I knew this woman too well, or rather the girl she'd once been.

"That's the thing. I was going to go to the next town over and stay in a hotel."

"Why?" I'd been about to put the truck in gear, but I paused, swiveling to look at her fully.

"I wanted the house to myself, and my brother Ian and Jane are there. I didn't know they'd still be here. I think maybe they're to-gether, and I don't want to spoil their time. They'll have all kinds of questions, and I don't want to explain."

I looked away from her, staring out the driver's side window at the snow falling thick and heavy. I could do the legwork and get Thea set up with a rental. Hell, I could even loan her one of my cars, but I didn't want her driving in this. I sure as hell didn't want to drive too far in it. It was late, and I was tired. I had takeout waiting at home.

"You can stay at my place."

Her eyes widened when I swung back to look at her. "What?"

"Just offering. There's no easy way to set up a rental at this hour. I can loan you a car, but the weather is shit, and it's just going to get worse tonight. I can crash on the couch, and you can sleep in my bed. As you can see, I'm on call tonight. We'll probably get a few more calls, but it shouldn't be too busy."

We stared at each other with the sound of the heater vents blowing and the snow striking against the windshield. After a long moment, she nodded. "Okay."

Then I surprised myself. "You just have to explain to me why the hell you're up here trying to hide out right before Christmas."

Thea pressed her lips together in a line. I knew what that meant. She was feeling stubborn. Fuck it. I might as well get the scoop on her life. Until now, she'd been this distant high school memory that I didn't let myself think about all that much. But I'd never stopped missing her. I'd always wondered if she'd ever come back to town. After what happened with her family, I knew she came to town now and then, but we'd never crossed paths.

"Okay," she finally said. "It'll be good to catch up."

I chuckled. "All right. Let's get your car to the garage."

We drove through downtown Haven's Bay, past where my dad's old garage was. Thea gestured toward it. "Aren't we stopping there?"

"Nope. That's only one location. We've expanded."

"Really?"

"Oh, yeah."

"Like how much?"

"We have two garages here and locations in eight nearby communities."

"You're a chain?"

I chuckled. "Yep. We're a chain, and I live right down the road from your old house."

Her laugh was dry. "Wow." After a pause, she added, "It's good to see you, Joe."

"You too."

"Really?"

My blinker was loud in the small space when I slowed to turn into the new garage. "Really," I said firmly.

"Wow." When I glanced over, she was looking around the large parking area.

"It's much bigger than the original garage."

"If you own all these garages, how come you're doing night duty?"

"Because I always cover it during the holidays. That's how my staff stay loyal," I offered with a shrug.

A few moments later, I'd pulled into one of the large garage bays. After I got her car situated, I took her on a little tour, ending at my office. "Here's my office." I gestured her through the door.

"Oh, you have an office?" she teased.

I rolled my eyes, flicking the lights on as she looked around. When she stopped to look at me, it suddenly felt as if a slingshot sped me back in time. Her tousled brown hair and big blue eyes were emblazoned in my memories.

This girl. I'd had the worst crush on her.

So bad. It was kind of embarrassing to think about it now.

She blinked up at me before she whispered, "I'm sorry."

"For what, sweetheart?"

She took a shuddery breath. Her lips curled down on one side. "Because my dad was an asshole, and I didn't have enough confidence to tell him to fuck off."

"We were sixteen. I get it."

I couldn't resist lifting a hand and brushing her damp, messy locks off her cheek.

"I know, but still. You always were that guy to me."

I arched a brow in question. "What do you mean?"

"I never really loved anybody the way I loved you. I could blame it on being young, but you were really good to me, Joe."

"I tried to be."

My voice was husky and had a ragged edge. I wanted to hide that, but I'd never been good at hiding much around Thea. We were standing in my office, for god's sake, and everything fell away. The mask slipped off.

I didn't remember where we were or any of my old resentment. All I wanted was to kiss her.

She was just a girl standing in front of a boy, a boy who really, *really* liked her and probably still loved her. Maybe that was faded and old, and maybe I was jaded, but none of that mattered right now. The air around us felt electrified as we stared at each other.

"Tell me something," I murmured, forcing myself to ask a question I didn't really want to know the answer to.

"What?" she whispered.

"Are you seeing someone?"

Her answer was instant. "No. Are you?"

I shook my head slowly. I expected her to be the sensible one, but she wasn't. She placed her palm on my chest where my jacket hung open. My heart kicked toward her palm, almost as if it were trying to break through my ribs. Just like the rest of me, my heart knew Thea.

I dipped my head just when she arched up toward me. Our lips collided, and it felt as if sparks leaped between us. My hand slid through her damp locks to palm her cheek. The second my lips met hers, I needed more.

Her tongue darted out to glide against mine, and our kiss went from a subtle taste to hot, openmouthed, and messy. By the time I broke away for air, my heartbeat was thundering, and my cock was thick and swollen, my arousal impatient.

Thea's eyes opened as she dragged in a breath. Her eyes were hazed with passion. We stared at each other.

"Oh," she finally said.

"Oh, is right."

Suddenly, there was a pounding on the front door down the hallway.

"Fuck, I forgot to turn off the alarm."

I spun away, striding quickly down the hallway to the front to see Howard Walker, the police chief, grinning through the windows.

"Forget the alarm?" he asked through the glass.

"I did," I called, relieved Thea hadn't followed me out here. "Sorry about that. Need to come in?"

"Nah, I was right down the road. Don't worry about it. Catch you later." He waved and jogged back toward his cruiser.

Thea was waiting inside my office, her hand curled on the edge of the doorframe. "Was that the police?"

"Oh, yeah. It was Howard Walker. He's the police chief now. I'm sure you remember the name."

Her cheeks flushed as she nodded. "Of course, I do. Sorry I distracted you."

"I guess we're even." I chuckled. "Come on, let's go."

Without thinking, I reached for her hand. As soon as we touched, I expected her to pull away, but she didn't. She laced her fingers through mine, and it felt exactly right.

I had been the forbidden boy for her in high school, but that wasn't why I'd asked her out back then. I'd really liked her. She'd helped me out in math class. Of course, teenage me also thought she was totally hot. We had that rare kind of chemistry. It flared hot, but it was also easy. She was comfortable to be around.

Once we were back in the tow truck, she commented, "If this is weird now—" She gestured vaguely in the direction of the garage. "Now that we have kissed, I can find a place to stay."

"It's not weird. I'll crash on the couch. Plus, I picked up a pizza before I got the call to pick you up. Let's go back and eat, and we can catch up. We've got twelve years to cover."

Thea's throaty laughter filled the small truck cab. We smiled at each other while the garage door rolled up.

"Do you park this at home?"

"I always keep one tow truck there, even when I'm not covering emergency calls. That way, if something happens, I don't have to race downtown. It's just a backup." As I turned onto the road that would lead us back through town and to my place, I jumped in with my questions. "I know you're not with anybody, but were you married, divorced? What's the scoop?"

"I had one bad engagement, and then I swore off men. I haven't really dated since then. I finally decided to give it a shot again." She let out a gusty sigh. "He turned out to be a real jerk, and I just found out."

"Found out what?"

A deeper sigh followed. "He never stopped seeing other people, and I feel like such an idiot."

"You're better off learning that now, right?"

My heart twisted a little. I didn't like how cynical and resigned she sounded.

"What about you?"

"Not married, not engaged. But I have a little boy."

"You're a father? Oh, wow. And you're not with——?"

I shook my head quickly. "Definitely not."

"Are things okay? Is he home with you tonight?"

"Nope. We have shared custody, but he's with his mom this week."

"What happened? I mean, you're definitely a loyal guy, so I'm trying to figure out why you're not married since you have a son."

"It was never even serious. All it takes is one night to make a baby."

Chapter Three

THEA

"How old is your son?" I heard myself asking, my mind trying to wrap itself around this detail.

"Six," Joe replied.

"What's his name?"

He slid his gaze to mine. "Joe."

I laughed softly.

"We call him Joey."

"That's what you used to go by."

"I know." He grinned as he looked back at the road. "I'm older now."

"Are you wiser?" I teased lightly.

His lips kicked up on one side, and my belly did a little flip. I tore my eyes away, looking around downtown Haven's Bay again. "It's just as pretty as I remembered."

"Do you miss Maine?"

Another rush of emotion hit me, and I had to clear my throat before I could answer. "I do. I come up a few times a year now."

"I think I saw you at the grocery store once."

"You did? How come you didn't say hi?" I looked back toward him.

His shoulder fell from a shrug. "I don't know. You were with Audrey. I think I had Joey with me. It didn't seem like good timing."

My heart twisted sharply in my chest. Because that hurt. "It's good to see you, Joe. I would have loved to have seen you sooner."

"Well, you're seeing me now. Audrey's married to Dallas, I heard. I've seen him a few times around town and ran into both of them at Emile's once. I hear Sasha and Noah got married too."

"They did. They got married last summer."

"I know. The reception was a big deal in town."

"Do you have all the gossip on my family?" I teased, trying to keep my tone light.

Joe chuckled as he turned onto the road that would lead us past my family's house. I was about to find out where he lived now.

"Haven's Bay is still a small town, Thea. It's not like I have to fish for the information."

"I know, I know. Sorry, that was weird."

"It wasn't weird. I always wondered how you were doing. What do you do?"

"For work, you mean?"

"Yes."

"I'm a lawyer."

"That's what you wanted to do. Good for you." His tone was warm, but I felt strange inside.

"I actually achieved one thing I set out to do," I said, my tone feeling scratchy in my throat.

"I'm sorry about your mom." His words were soft.

"Thanks." My chest got tight again, and I took a quick breath.

"She always liked you."

Joe nodded. "How are things for you and your brothers with everything that went down with your dad?"

"Ah, that ugly story. We're good actually. No love lost there. My dad was an asshole," I said flatly.

"Well, I knew that." His tone was dry and resigned. "It was kind of a shock to realize he was a criminal too."

I took a breath. "Yeah."

"Do you stay in touch with him?"

"He's in jail, Joe."

"I know, but there are phones and letters."

I shrugged. "Not much. None of us were close to him before he got charged. It was kind of a turning point for our family and brought me closer to my brothers. The only thing we kept was the house. Ian and Dallas paid off everybody that dad owed money to. Ugh, did he owe your garage any money?"

Joe's dry laugh rustled in his throat. "No, he didn't use our garage, Thea."

I didn't realize what I was doing until it happened, but I reached over and curled my hand over his where it rested on the gearshift. "I'm sorry."

His gaze slid sideways to mine. I wasn't quite sure how to read it in the dim light. "It's okay. Like I said, we were young. Your dad was an asshole. That's the story."

Of all the people I expected to run into tonight, Joe hadn't even crossed my mind. Now, he was a father. I felt like I should have known that somehow.

When we drove past my family's house, I glanced sideways. The lights were glowing in the snowy darkness. The snow had eased up slightly, but the roads were still slick.

"So, I saw Jane and Ian, by the way."

"You did?"

"Yup. She also bent her tire rim, and I towed her car."

"Seriously?"

Joe flashed me a grin. "Sure did. I thought they had a thing going."

"I was hoping so. That's why I didn't want to show up unannounced at the house. She just moved to Boston. I let her know she could stay at the house for a few weeks, and apparently, Ian's there too."

"Aside from not wanting to interrupt them, why don't you want to stay there?"

I let out a sigh as he turned on his blinker. "Oh wow, you're just down the road."

"Yep. This lot was mostly wooded. It still is, but I built a house here."

"That's awesome, Joe. I know you love the ocean. You must be doing well for yourself because this property could not have been cheap."

He shrugged. "I never wanted to be rich, but I'm comfortable, and I love Haven's Bay. It was nice to be able to build this place."

"And it's just you here?"

"Me, and Joey when he stays with me."

The driveway was long, like most of those on this stretch of road. In another moment, we passed through a cluster of trees. When they opened up, lights were blazing through the darkness and snow. Joe slowed to turn around a circular driveway, pulling up to a garage and tapping a small button clipped on the visor in his truck.

By the time Joe had parked and led me into his house, my nerves felt stripped raw. This entire situation was strange and unexpected. And that crazy kiss had set my body spiraling. I felt like a pinball machine with a muddle of emotion, desire, and surprise bouncing around.

His dog, Dexter, greeted us when we entered from the garage. "Do you recognize him?" Joe teased as he scratched behind Dexter's ears.

"I don't know. All I saw was a dog-shaped shadow running across the road." I smiled down at his dog.

Dexter was white with two large brown splotches on his body. Half of his face was brown and the other white. He was very friendly, wiggling and wagging and circling me with excitement.

"Easy, buddy, she just walked in."

Joe had my bag in his hand and set it by the door. "You can hang up your jacket and leave your boots here."

We walked into a small entryway between the garage and kitchen. After I took care of my jacket and boots, Joe took me on a quick house tour with Dexter following along.

"This is a really nice place, Joe."

His home was a low-slung ranch-style—not too big but not too small. There was a beautiful open living room with a vaulted ceiling. The view tonight was of the darkness and blowing snow, but I knew the ocean would be visible during the daylight. His home had a modern, clean feel to it.

"Is gray your favorite color?" I teased.

Joe caught my eyes, rolling his in return. "My sister picked out all the colors and decided to keep it simple."

"It's nice." There were a few splashes of color with a deep maroon rug on the hardwood floor.

An archway from the living room led into a kitchen with modern, stainless-steel appliances and a cute breakfast nook by the windows. Down the hallway were three bedrooms and a bath. His son's bedroom was cheerfully decorated.

"I love the bed," I offered with a smile, gesturing to the car-shaped bed.

He shrugged. "Also, my sister."

"How is Stacy?" I asked as we walked across the hallway to the master bedroom.

"She's good. She lives in Brunswick now. She does all the accounting for us, so it works out really well."

"Is she married? Does she have kids?"

"No, and no. She babysits when I need it."

"Nice bedroom." I looked around the master bedroom.

Simply being near a bed with Joe had butterflies twirling in my belly again. Much of my dating relationship with Joe involved making out in cars. It had been maybe a full year that we pulled off all that sneaking around with my father getting grumpier and grumpier. He finally called a halt to it when we got caught making out in the parking lot behind Joe's garage.

My eyes took in the king-sized bed. It was low to the floor and built into the wall. There was a doorway to the side, which I presumed was a master bath.

My guess was confirmed when he said, "I even have my own bathroom. I don't really need it. Although I only have Joey half of the time, he makes a mess in the bathroom, so it is kind of nice. Now let's eat because I'm freaking starving. My pizza's probably cold, so I'm gonna throw it in the oven if you don't mind."

"Of course, I don't mind," I replied as I followed him into the kitchen. "You don't have to feed me."

His gaze slid sideways to mine. "I'm not so rude that I'd sit here and eat in front of you. Are you hungry?"

As if in answer, my belly rumbled, and he chuckled. He needed to stop smiling. His slow smiles were making my body go wild, and I still hadn't completely cooled down from that kiss back at the garage.

"Have a seat." He gestured toward the nook by the windows.

I slipped into the bench seat and looked around. "This is really cute, Joe," I called over.

He turned on the oven and pulled the pizza out of the box to place it onto a large baking sheet. "I like it," he replied after he closed the oven. "It's comfortable. That nook is a great place to have coffee in the morning."

"I bet." Snow swirled in the darkness beyond the windows, and the wind came in rolling gusts off the ocean.

"You'll get to see it tomorrow. Let's hope the snow lightens up before then."

All I could think about was the fact that I was spending the night alone in a house with Joe. I would have paid money for this in high school. While we ate, we chatted and caught up on life. All the while, an onslaught of memories rolled through me.

Every glance from him felt knowing. When I helped him clean up, the mere brush of his elbow against mine sent desire pinging through me. No matter how hard I tried, I couldn't forget that kiss.

Joe didn't even get another emergency call. "It's quiet tonight," he commented at one point.

"Were you expecting more calls?"

"It's hit or miss near the holidays. Most people aren't driving that late in this weather," he replied with a knowing look in my direction.

"I just needed a break."

We were sitting on the couch now, and Joe was maybe two feet away from me. The distance felt way too close and way too far all at the same time.

I made a quick decision. This might be one night, but I could use the kind of escape I hadn't had in years, probably since high school with this very guy. I angled toward him with my pulse galloping out of control.

"Let's have one night." My voice came out breathy although I was trying to be bold.

"What do you mean, Thea?"

I scooted closer, shimmying onto his lap so I was straddling him. "This," I said decisively before I leaned forward and kissed him again.

Chapter Four

JOE

With a lapful of Thea and her lips brushing across mine, the need I'd been trying to tamp down flared hot. Before I could think it through, I was sliding one palm down her back to lever her closer to me and lacing my fingers in her hair to angle her head to the side.

I fit my mouth over hers and took control of our kiss. Fuck me. Lightning sizzled through me. Ever since that kiss back at the garage, I'd been trying to get control of my need, all to no avail. My arousal had been at half-mast all evening. My cock swelled to an ache the moment her lips touched mine.

Thea was a drug, the very best kind for my body, the forbidden fruit. I'd fallen for her so hard in high school and pined for what we'd had after she broke it off. And here she was, kissing me, and there was absolutely no reason not to let this go further.

Maybe she wanted just one night, but I had other plans. We would start with one night, though.

She gasped when I slid my hands down her sides. Her skin was silky soft when I slipped a palm up and caught the hem of her shirt, letting it ride up around my wrist.

Fuck me. Kissing Thea was heaven. She tasted just like I remembered, a little sweet. Her lips were soft and plump as her tongue sensually glided against mine. She broke free, gulping in air. Her lips were swollen and kiss bitten as she stared at me.

"Is this crazy?" she rasped.

"Absolutely not."

She blinked, her lips curling in a slow, sensual smile.

"Let's get the practical matters out of the way first," I added.

She took another breath. "Practical?"

"I need to get a condom. Do you have any condoms?"

Her eyes widened slightly, and she let out a startled laugh. "No. Do you?"

I shook my head. "No, I'm not seeing

anyone, and I don't usually bring anyone here. We might have to take a drive."

Thea shook her head sharply. "I can't get pregnant."

"You can't?" I was jolted at this.

She nodded and took a quick breath. "I can't. I swear."

I had no idea how to respond to this. "Are you okay?" I pressed.

She swallowed, shrugging lightly. "Well, yes and no. I'd rather not talk about the whole thing right now. This isn't exactly a romantic conversation, you know," she added.

"I know." Her eyes were tight at the corners, and I sensed she was shutting me out.

"If you're worried about me not being clean, it's been a while." This whole conversation was strange. When we were together before, we were young and so into each other we didn't think much about serious matters. My father had given me a very stern lecture about condoms, and I always had them on me back then.

"Same," I said slowly.

"Okay, is there anything else practical that we missed?" Thea pressed.

No, but I was suddenly worried about her. I should have known this, and my heart felt a little funny. "Thea, if—"

She shook her head sharply. "Please, Joe, don't force me to talk about this now."

I brushed her hair back and nodded. I figured we would have to cross this bridge later. She lifted her hand, trailing her thumb along my jaw before she leaned forward to kiss me again.

Then I was breathing her in as our kiss went on and on. She shoved at my T-shirt, breaking free to murmur, "I need to feel your chest."

Our clothes came off in a tangled rush. Thea had filled out since high school, and her breasts were plump and bouncy.

"Fuck, sweetheart," I murmured, pressing greedy kisses along the side of her neck.

Her skin was flushed pink. She bit her lip as I trailed my knuckles down her breastbone and paused to undo the clasp of her bra. It fell to the sides, and her breasts bounced free.

She took a shaky breath. I cupped a breast, dragging my thumb across her already taut nipple. I watched as her eyes darkened and her hips rocked over the hard ridge of my arousal. I dipped my head to catch her nipple in my mouth, savoring the way she arched her back reflexively. I swirled my tongue around, sucking lightly and letting my teeth graze her nipple before I lifted my head.

She blinked, letting out a ragged gasp.

Thea was glorious, and I forgot how good it felt to be with her. She'd been the star of many fantasies, but if there were memories to doubt, high school memories were definitely those. It was so easy to view those years through a haze. We'd dated for six months in the open and six months surreptitiously. One whole year. I thought nothing could usurp just how hot those memories had burned.

Yet getting this chance with her was its own fuel to the fire burning inside me. It kindled higher and higher with every subtle response from her.

"Thea," I whispered.

She dragged her eyes open, and we stared at each other.

"Let's go to my bedroom."

She blinked again, looking a little confused. I decided to simply be honest. "All we ever got before were stolen moments. This night is ours. We even have a bed."

It felt as if our youthful selves—craving each other, loving each other, but being too young and stupid to really know how good it had been for us—rose like smoke in the air around us, that connection shimmering to life and taking shape at this moment.

Her lips curled into a slow, sensual smile, and fuck me, she bit her bottom lip again. Right on the corner. She had one tooth that was the tiniest bit crooked. I'd never forgotten how sexy it was when she bit her lip, and that tooth was a little kickstand on the corner.

"Okay," she whispered.

I palmed her cheek, giving her a fierce kiss. Just as she began to shimmy off my lap, I lifted her. We stood together, stumbling to the bedroom. It wasn't all that far, but we didn't make it quickly. We kept pausing to kiss, our hands mapping each other, stealing touches, reacquainting ourselves.

Her skin was still silky soft, and her curves were fuller. Something about her was more solid—not physically but just in her presence. She giggled when she bumped into the edge of my doorway and then rolled around it, leaning against the wall. Her bra had gotten lost on the floor somewhere between the couch and here. Her jeans were unbuttoned, and her breasts heaved with her laughter.

My heart gave a sweet twist as fierce tenderness stole through me. *That* girl, *my* girl, was here in my house. She was currently stringing kisses along my collarbone. Then she dragged her palm boldly over my cock.

That was a little different. She hadn't been bashful when she was young, but we'd been each other's first. That came with fumbling and uncertainty on both of our parts. Anyone who pretended that wasn't the case in their early experiences was a bald-faced liar as far as I was concerned.

I rested my palms on the wall, just above her shoulders, and dipped my head, pressing a kiss in that sweet dip at the base of her throat. When I lifted my head, she had stopped giggling.

"I'm glad you're here," I rasped.

I heard Dexter's tail thumping on the floor, just beyond the doorway. He had a preference for sleeping in the hallway. He liked to keep an eye on things.

"I think Dexter thinks you're talking to him," she offered.

I chuckled. "Yeah, well, I'm glad he's here too, but he can stay in the hallway."

I felt my lips kicking up at the corner as we stared at each other for a few beats. She lifted a hand, and her knuckles landed on my breastbone. She unfurled her palm, pressing it flat there.

"I'm glad I'm here too. It definitely wasn't something I was expecting."

"Sometimes, surprises are the best things."

Her eyes searched mine, and then we were kissing again. I peeled her jeans off. She tugged impatiently on the buttons of my fly, swearing when she caught a finger.

"Geez, Joe. These are stiff."

I laughed. "They're actually kind of new."

"I hate new jeans," she announced.

"They need a few more washings."

Her eyes swept up to mine. She was seated on the edge of my bed now, naked save for her bright pink cotton panties, which somehow suited her perfectly, and a pair of mismatched socks. Socks weren't something Thea had ever thought much about.

I let my eyes trail upward. When they collided with hers again, her cheeks flushed a deeper shade of pink.

"Fuck, Thea. You're more beautiful than I remembered."

Uncertainty flickered in her eyes, and I wanted to punch every man who had put any doubt there.

"You're not so bad yourself," she teased slightly.

"I try to keep up, you know." When I patted my stomach, she rolled her eyes.

"You actually have a six-pack, Joe. You were all lanky in high school, but you're definitely not anymore."

"Sweetheart, my job is pretty physical sometimes."

"So you don't work out?" she asked lightly.

I shook my head. Because Lord knows I didn't need to. She dipped her head, stringing kisses just above the open fly of my jeans. Each spot where her lips landed felt like a hot brand on my skin with flames licking over the surface and scattering sparks through me.

Impatient and frankly needing something to keep me under control, I nudged her back on the bed. Then I shucked my jeans, keeping my briefs on.

Thea shimmied back a little further, and I paused, pressing one knee into the mattress between her ankles. Her hair was tousled around her shoulders, and she was resting on one hand as she shifted back, wobbling and almost tumbling to the side. It wasn't graceful, and it was perfect.

I slid one palm up the inside of her calf, and her eyes locked to mine. Her mouth parted slightly when she sucked in a sharp breath of air.

She said something, but I couldn't even absorb it. I leaned over, dusting kisses over her belly, and she trembled under my touch. I slid my palm farther up along her leg, pushing her knee to the side. I cupped her mound, only to discover her bright pink cotton panties were damp. Her hips bucked reflexively into my touch.

Holy hell. I wanted to take this slow, to savor every second of it, but I could hardly think over the roar of desire crashing through me. I teased my fingers over the cotton, and she murmured something followed with, "Please, Joe." And then she said, "Don't make me beg."

I chuckled against her belly. Lifting my head, I replied, "You just did."

She had enough sass to roll her eyes. I shoved that cotton out of the way, dipping my fingers through her slippery wet folds, savoring her ragged gasp and the arch of her hips into my touch. After that, everything blurred.

I dragged her panties off, impatient to taste her. As I sank two fingers into her again, her salty musk filled my senses. She bucked roughly, ruining any attempt at finesse. I gripped her hip with one hand, swirling my tongue around her clit and lightly sucking it. I could feel her about to spin loose, to crash over that edge as her whole body trembled. I needed to be inside her before that happened.

Thea was on the same page, ordering, "Joe, come here," in a raspy but demanding whisper.

I rose, looking down at her. She impatiently shoved at my briefs. She almost knocked me off the bed when I rolled to the side to try to shimmy them off and give her an assist.

We were laughing by the time I recovered from that. Then her eyes were dark on mine, and she straddled me, saying, "My turn."

She rose over me, and I held her still for a moment, muttering, "Hold on." I shifted until my back was propped against the pillows.

She followed my motion, her eyes holding mine. Her lips were kiss swollen. With my heartbeat kicking hard and fast, I watched as she rose, reaching between us. I felt the slick kiss of her core before she slid down slowly, sheathing me in her silky, clenching channel.

I had to grit my teeth and cling to the frayed threads of my control. She made this little humming sound when she settled her hips down, seating herself fully. She moved to rise up again, and I murmured, "Wait."

Her lashes lifted. Releasing her hip, I slid my palm up her back, levering her closer. Eyes wide open, I brought her mouth to mine. We tumbled into a kiss, and I felt like I'd finally come home.

Chapter Five

THEA

I felt surrounded, inside and out, by Joe. He filled me completely, the stretch of it intoxicating and decadent. His tongue commanded mine in a slow dance. We broke free and gulped in air.

Somehow, even though I was riding him, he controlled every second of this with slow nudges into me. As we rocked, my breasts pressed against his chest. He took deep sips from my mouth between slow nips and kisses.

My release was spiraling. I felt as if I were spinning tighter and tighter inside, the pleasure ricocheting through me from the tension as it built and built until I could hardly bear it. The pressure was exquisite, and then he did something magical with his thumbs. The coil of tension snapped loose, crashing in intense waves. Aftershocks rippled through me as I gasped for air and chanted his name.

I distantly heard him cry out roughly with the gruff whisper of my name following as he shuddered against me. I could feel the hard press of his palm flat between my shoulder blades and the heat of his release filling me.

I was boneless against him, and his grip eased as he held me close. Our hearts beat in tune with each other as our breathing slowed. Eventually, I felt his hand start to slide up and down my back before he smoothed through the tangled mess of my hair.

I had no idea how much time had passed since I'd straddled his lap in the living room. We could've been on another planet for all I was concerned.

I reluctantly lifted my head and dragged my eyes open. His head was resting against the headboard, his eyes on me, the look contained there was dark and intimate. My breath caught in my throat, and my heartbeat lunged all over again.

"Oh, wow," I breathed with a blink.

His mouth curled up in a slow, sensual smile. "Wow is right."

To my surprise, Joe tugged me into the

shower, where the hot water and steam cocooned us. After that, we crawled into bed. When I said I wanted more pizza, he went and got it. I admired just how great his body was as he unabashedly walked to the kitchen bare-ass naked. He returned with the pizza and set the box on the bed between us. We ate cooled pizza while the television rumbled in the background.

He fielded two emergency calls although he didn't end up having to go anywhere.

At one point, I said, "If you need to go, you can. I'm sure Dexter will watch over me. I won't steal anything."

He grinned. "I'm not leaving unless I have to."

We fell asleep together, and I savored it in a way I couldn't have imagined. Wrapped in Joe's strong embrace, I almost wondered if I would wake up and realize it was all a dream.

Chapter Six

JOE

Waking up with Thea was the manifestation of my high school fantasy. Because my habits were deeply ingrained, I woke when it was still dark. Thea was curled up warm and soft beside me. Her knee was thrown over my thigh, and her head tucked into the crook of my shoulder.

I took a deep breath, letting it out quietly. I didn't want to wake her. I didn't want to snap this moment. Her breathing stayed even and steady. My pulse had initially kicked off at a rapid pace once my awareness flickered into wakefulness, but it slowed. As good as this felt and as exciting as it was, a sense of peace came with it.

Of course, my body had ideas. I'd woken

fully aroused. I chuckled to myself. That woke Thea.

"What?" she murmured, her voice roughened with sleep.

"You. Us. Here," I explained.

She shifted, and her knee brushed against my arousal. "Oh, is that what's funny?"

"Something like that."

My arm was curled around her shoulders, and I moved my hand up, sifting my fingers through her hair.

"It's windy out," she murmured into the darkness.

"I think it's still snowing."

I could hear the barely-there sound of the wind blowing the snow against the house. It wasn't like rain. There was a soft brushing quality to it, but I knew the sound well because I'd lived on the coast of Maine for my entire life.

"Do you normally wake up early?" she asked.

"Yeah, you?"

Her chin shifted in a nod against my shoulder. "I always have, even in high school."

"I used to sleep in, but that habit has been thoroughly broken."

"How?"

"I start work early. Before I took over

management at the business, I was more frequently on duty for the emergency service too. I'm usually up by five, whether I want to be or not," I explained.

I could feel the curve of her smile against my shoulder. Something about this conversation felt like a lasso cinching around my heart—the intimacy of it, the mundane details of our lives, all these things we didn't know about each other. I knew Thea, but then I didn't.

"What are you doing today?" I asked.

"Well, now, I don't know."

I felt her shift, rising up on an elbow. My fingers slid through her hair as she moved. "I have no idea."

"Really?"

She rested her palm on my chest and her chin upon that. "Are you working?"

"I'll probably go in just to check on things, but we're closed except for emergency service for the two weeks around the holidays."

She seemed surprised by this, her brows hitching up. "Oh, we stay busy. The admin offices are open, and the emergency appointments keep the garage busy. My dad always did that."

"I don't remember that."

"There was no reason for you to know. You gonna go see your brother and Jane today?"

Thea took a breath, letting it out in a soft sigh. "I'll go at Christmas, like we planned. But no sooner."

"How come?"

"I just don't want to get into all of it."

"Tell me what happened," I pressed.

She was quiet for a moment, and then her stomach rumbled. I let out a hearty laugh.

"How about we have some coffee and breakfast? I even have a waffle maker."

Thea's giggle tightened that lasso around my heart. "Yeah, let's do that."

THEA

Joe insisted we shower first. Once we were in there, he started kissing me while the water ran down around us. It was a blur of warmth and need and lingering touches as we explored each other. Lifting me against the wall, he thrust into me, and I trembled all over, the pleasure nearly undoing me.

Jesus, there was Joe in high school, and then there was this Joe—all man, all hot and sexy and magic for my body. This man knew how to make my body sing. He played me like his own personal instrument. I came in a noisy rush, and his forehead fell to mine as he shuddered against me, filling me with the heat of his release.

My knees were wobbly as he eased me

down. "Easy there, now," he murmured, one hand firmly steadying me by the hip and the other at my shoulders.

"Joe," I managed in a breathy reply.

Once I had my balance, he caught my lips in a lingering kiss as he drew away, murmuring, "I could get used to this."

That was the problem. I could get used to it too.

———

"How can I help?" I asked a short while later as we stood in the kitchen.

Joe was wearing a pair of jeans and a blinding white T-shirt, which only set off his muscled chest and the olive bronze tinge of his skin.

"You want to make coffee? I promise the waffles are good, but I use a box mix."

I felt my lips tugging into a wide smile. Breakfast with my high school sweetheart after last night was about the best thing ever.

"Okay. I'll do the coffee."

Joe pointed me to where the coffee beans were. I ground the coffee and started a pot. A few minutes later, I watched him as he prepped the waffles in a bright blue waffle maker.

"That's cute," I commented.

He shrugged. "My mom got it for me. Joey loves waffles, so when he's here on the weekends, that's what we have for breakfast."

"Tell me about him."

Joe pointed at a photo I'd already noticed. Crossing the kitchen to where it sat on the windowsill, I felt my heart clench as I studied it. It was Joe with his son, a little boy who looked just like him. We'd gone to school together, starting in kindergarten. I knew what he'd looked like as a little boy.

"Oh, wow. He looks so much like you did."

He came to stand behind me, his palm landing between my shoulder blades. My body was attenuated to his touch, a shiver chasing over my skin and my heart kicking hard against my ribs.

"You're not the first to say that," he offered dryly.

"What's he like?"

"Full of energy. He's mostly good, but he also has, well, a contrary streak."

"No way," I teased. "You were never like that."

Joe rolled his eyes, and my heart thumped when I turned and peered up at him. He'd definitely had a stubborn streak when he was little and had gotten in trouble at school on occasion.

"Is it hard?" I asked.

He knew what I was asking even though I didn't clarify—having a kid and not being with his mom. "Yes and no. Yes, because it's never what I would have chosen. No, because it was a one-night stand, literally. We are not cut out to be in a relationship. We manage the co-parenting thing okay. It takes a lot of grace and a lot of biting my tongue, but we do all right."

"How often do you have him?"

"She has him mostly during the weeks unless something comes up, and I have him most weekends. We worked out a schedule, and we stick to it, for the most part."

"I bet you're a good dad," I said, meaning it and ignoring the achy thump of my heart.

The coffeemaker beeped, and we turned together. I needed the distraction. Crossing the kitchen, I poured coffee for both of us. Joe finished getting the waffles ready. After that, the conversation turned to lighter topics.

I was absorbing the morning and what it felt like to see Joe after all these years. To have last night with him was startling. This morning, my heart felt as if it were flailing. I was set adrift on emotional waters I didn't know how to navigate.

Joe reached across the table, catching my hand in his as I felt his knee press against mine. His somber gaze met mine, earnest and intense. "Here's the thing, Thea. I know last night might feel like a fluke, but I don't want it to be."

I thought my heart might crack my ribs as it felt caught in the wind and yanked upward with hope sending flares into the sky. "What?" I whispered.

"I loved you before. And it's been a long time, but it just feels right with you," he continued, oblivious to the cacophony in my body.

Oh. My. God. That was the thing. It did feel right with Joe. I'd loved him before too. It was youthful and almost saccharine sweet, the way only young love could be. I'd been so crushed when my father forbade me from dating him.

Despite the joy rushing through me and my heart going wild, doubts and uncertainty were the name of the game when it came to my brain and romance. "But, Joe, I don't live here." I heard myself saying.

Joe was undeterred. "We'll figure it out. What's the harm in trying? Boston's only a few hours away. I know that you know that this thing that we have doesn't come along very often. In fact, I've only felt it with you." His eyes searched mine. "And don't lie to me about that, please."

Tears rushed to my eyes, and my throat felt tight. I couldn't lie, not to Joe. "I won't lie."

His steady, intent gaze held mine, and I took a quick breath.

"I know it's not something that comes along very often."

"So?" he prompted.

Hope sent up a few more flares, and I felt my lips curling into a slow smile. "Okay, we can try."

"We have one pretty big thing working in our favor."

"We do?" While I was feeling wildly, ridiculously hopeful, and wistful, it all seemed too good, like it couldn't really work out for us. I'd let Joe go in my mind years ago. I'd felt like I had no choice.

"This." He gestured back and forth between us.

I suddenly felt like my teenage self, that young girl who loved a boy so, so very much. A boy who made her feel safe and loved. That boy was now a man. His presence that had once felt protective and youthful was sharpened and honed. I thought maybe this was crazy, but maybe we *did* have a chance.

"Okay," I managed after a deep breath.

"I think you should just stay here."

"What?" I squeaked.

"Where are you going to go? You're being all weird about going to your family's place so stay with me. Joey has Christmas with his mom this year. It's just me."

"What about your parents?"

"I'll go see them on Christmas Day. I'm assuming you'll go see your family."

I nodded. "I don't want us to be a secret." I surprised myself with that.

Joe's eyes flew wide. "Ah, well, now that kind of surprises me."

I shrugged. "My dad's in jail, and my mom's gone. I don't care what anyone thinks."

He smiled, dipping his chin in a quick nod. "I do need to take it slow with Joey."

"Oh, I understand that part, but we'll figure it out. That'll be the upside to me living in Boston."

His eyes warmed as he cocked his head to the side, considering me. "Good point."

A moment later, when he leaned across the table to kiss me, it all felt so right.

Chapter Eight

JOE

The following days leading up to Christmas were some of the best I'd had in years. It was strange and incredible to have Thea with me. Even though we were at my house and I was covering the emergency call service, which meant I got called out several times a day, it somehow felt like we were in a bubble.

It was familiar, but not. Thea was back in Haven's Bay with me. Since she was hiding out from her brother and trying not to blow up his spot with Jane, it was kind of funny to sneak around town. We'd agreed we weren't going to keep us a secret, but we'd wait to break the news to family until after the holidays.

We stocked up on groceries, and I learned

Thea had gone from being a pretty good cook in high school to a kick-ass cook now. Every time I had to leave to deal with a car emergency, she made sure I had food when I got back. Dexter loved it because he was never alone. I got to discover her all over again.

We drove through town one day because Thea insisted I get a tree. I usually took my son to my parents' for Christmas, so I hadn't decorated. She held my hand as I drove through town. It was all very picturesque, and it felt like I was seeing it through fresh eyes even though I'd spent every Christmas of my life in this town. Thea's joy at being home was contagious.

"How much time have you spent here since you moved away?"

"The last few years I've come up during the holidays and in the summer. We've all been taking turns getting the house back up to speed. Ian's been doing a lot of work, so I'm curious to see it tomorrow."

I slowed to turn into the Christmas tree lot. Lights were strung around the edges of the area. "You know there aren't many trees left," I commented as we walked through a few minutes later.

She shrugged. "We'll get a straggler and make it beautiful. They even sell lights here."

I let her pick out the tree, which was lopsided but plenty green. That night, she happily strung lights on it.

"Merry Christmas," she called.

Turning, I saw she'd hung a sprig of mistletoe in the entrance into the kitchen. Dexter's tail thumped on the floor when I dipped my head for a kiss.

Chapter Nine

THEA

A month later

I was nervous, *way* more nervous than I should have been. Joe was coming to Boston for the first time to see me, and I didn't know what to think.

Walking around my small apartment, I kept checking on things. I fluffed the pillows on the couch for probably the tenth time. I jumped when the doorbell rang and smoothed my hands on my jeans before practically sprinting to the front door. With my hand clasped around the doorknob, I took a deep breath.

I must have waited for a few beats too

long because Joe's voice came through the door. "I can hear you breathing, Thea."

I could hear the smile in his voice, and I laughed softly as I opened the door. The second my eyes landed on him, my pulse lunged. He stepped through the doorway, dropped his bag to the floor, and pulled me into his strong embrace. I felt startlingly alive as if I'd been electrified. At the same time, the tension coiled inside me eased, and I started to relax.

Joe had this weird opposite effect on me, where it was just so amazing to see him, so good that my hormones were always super excited about it, yet it also felt right and easy. I could relax and be myself with him in a way that I wasn't with anyone.

He held me, just long enough for me to absorb the imprint of him, then stepped back. His eyes skated over my face. "Hey, sweetheart. You look nervous."

I cast him a sheepish smile. "I was, but now it's okay because you're here."

Closing the door behind him, I swung my arm in an arc. "This is my apartment."

Joe stepped past me, his alert gaze arcing about the small space. "I like it." His eyes made their way back to mine.

"It's small, but rentals cost a fortune in Boston," I commented.

I lived in a walk-up on the second floor of a cute little brownstone right near the Charles River. Like most walk-up apartments, it was created from reconfigured space in the original home. This floor had a small efficiency kitchen with a living room and a bedroom with the bathroom off to the side. The high ceilings created a sense of spaciousness.

"How was your drive?"

"It's a pretty drive from Maine down here, so it was easy."

I glanced at the clock in the kitchen. "Do you want to eat here or go out? It's your call since you're the one who had to drive."

Joe's eyes lingered on my face. "Sweetheart, I just want to be with you, so whatever is easier for you. Although, you know I like to eat."

Heat bloomed through me while my heart thumped in reaction to his comment. "I do. I thought maybe we could go to an Italian place. You always tell me that's the one thing we don't have enough of in Haven's Bay. There are tons of Italian restaurants in Boston."

"Let's do it. Then we can come back here and just hang out."

Joe caught my hand and reeled me to him when I started to turn away.

"What?" I asked breathlessly.

"It's just good to see you."

Then he was kissing me, and I forgot to be nervous about anything. Kisses with Joe were like diving into flames. Everything he did ignited the fire higher and higher.

Moments later after he'd fetched his bag from the floor and put it in my bedroom, we walked outside.

"Where did you park?" I asked as we descended the stairs together.

He gestured at his SUV in front of the building. "I scored a good spot."

"I actually have driveway parking, so you can pull into the spot behind me."

"You have two spots?"

"Yup, serious luxury," I teased.

I waited while he parked behind me, smiling at his Maine license plate. A minute later, his hand was curled around mine, and we were walking down the sidewalk together. That feeling that still was fresh but familiar stole through me. Being with Joe simply felt *good*.

In the month since Christmas, I'd gone up to Haven's Bay every other weekend. Joe had offered to come down here, but I preferred going up there. It was a respite from the hustle and bustle of the city, and I enjoyed being in my hometown in a way I hadn't anticipated.

One major bonus was I didn't have to worry about where to stay because I always stayed with Joe.

———

Joe leaned back in his chair, his half-grin sending my belly into a series of somersaults.

"That was damn good," he said, patting his belly, which was a drum-tight wall of muscle.

I laughed. "I thought you'd like it."

"Do you come here often?" he asked, glancing around.

I'd brought him to a small Italian restaurant on a corner near my apartment. It wasn't the fanciest, but the food was fresh and delicious.

"I don't eat out too much because Boston is filled with amazing restaurants, and I could go broke quickly."

"Maybe I should come see you more often," he teased.

His gaze sobered as he leaned his elbows on the table and reached for one of my hands. I totally had a thing for Joe's hands. Gah! They were like all of him, lean and muscled. He definitely had working hands, and by some miracle, they were rarely dirty. He told me he occasionally still did mechanic work but didn't have much time for it. He also claimed to have the best soap ever to keep his hands clean from the mechanic filth, as he put it.

The calloused surface of his thumb brushing on my wrist sent fire sparks skittering over my skin and heat spiraling in its wake. I tried to focus.

"I like coming to Haven's Bay," I answered honestly. I really did.

"I know, but I don't want you to feel like you have to come to me all the time," he pressed.

"I don't feel like I have to," I insisted.

"Okay, let me rephrase. It's important for me to be putting as much effort into *us* as you are. Plus, good food is a bonus. I've probably eaten at every restaurant in the area surrounding Haven's Bay a few hundred times."

"I know Joe but—"

He squeezed my hand. "Thea, you're starting to fret, aren't you?"

Joe knew me so well. Even now. He'd known me better than anyone in high school and that knowledge carried into the present. He tuned in to me easily.

I *had* been fretting about how we were going to do this. We hadn't said the words, but I knew I loved Joe. I had already fallen for him. All over again. It wasn't exactly a hardship. In fact, it was very easy to love Joe. He was the kind of man just about anyone would want—attentive, caring, and smoking hot in bed.

But his life was in Haven's Bay, and I was here in Boston. I didn't want to be yoked to my job, but I'd never considered my career path taking me back to Haven's Bay. I needed to figure it out. I didn't want to move just because of Joe, but then, I fretted maybe that was the very best reason to move.

"Thea?" he prompted again, his thumb brushing over the back of my hand.

I brought my focus to him. "How do you know I was fretting?"

"Sweetheart, the gears in your brain are practically loud enough for me to hear."

Heat flared in my cheeks. "Okay, so I was fretting."

"Didn't we already have this conversation? We'll see how it plays out. People regularly commute to Boston for work. They drive down to Wells and take the train. We can figure it out, or maybe I could move."

I shook my head swiftly. To me, that was out of the question. He had a son who lived in Haven's Bay. It didn't make sense for him to move away.

Joe distracted me when his thumb curled inward and teased on the inside of my palm. His voice was low and gravelly with his reply. "Thea, let's just—" he began before shaking his head sharply. "Stop worrying," he said more forcefully.

He leaned across the table and pressed his lips firmly to mine. It felt as if flames danced over my lips when he drew away.

"Okay," I said.

"Sweetheart, if all we have to worry about is a few hours between us, that's not much. Everything else is good. Really good. Unless you're not telling me something."

I blinked as emotion crashed through me. "No, everything's really good."

His lips curled into a slow smile, and my belly swooped. "Okay, then. Now, I need dessert."

"I thought you were full," I teased.

"I am, but they've got some kind of double chocolate mousse thing. I can't *not* get it."

I giggled, and he squeezed my hand. Joe had this way of knowing just when to lighten the moment with me, and it always worked. I loved him all the more for it because my emotions got ahead of my thoughts too often.

"I love you." Speaking of my emotions getting ahead of things. Those words spilled out.

He'd flipped open the small dessert menu tucked between the condiments in the center of the table, and his eyes whipped up to mine, going dark. His gaze was fierce. "I love you too."

"You didn't—"

He shook his head, and I fell quiet. "There's nothing wrong with saying how I feel, just like you did."

"Is it too soon?" I asked.

"There you go fretting again," he teased. "Maybe if we hadn't known each other before, but I don't think there are rules on how fast to fall in love. It didn't make it any less meaningful before. Sure, we were young and maybe a little stupid, but we didn't break up. Your dad broke us up because he was a controlling asshole. I still think he's an asshole."

I pressed my lips together before a smile

unfurled across my face. "I know. It's just this time—" I stopped myself.

Joe leaned over again, kissing me quickly once more. "Sweetheart, what the hell happened? Who broke your heart? Because you are filled with doubts. That's always where you go."

"Well, I don't know how this is going to work," I protested.

"I'm not really sure either, but maybe we can just enjoy what's good."

I hadn't filled in all the gaps for him when I told him why I was avoiding Ian and Jane before. I'd just told him I'd gotten dumped, and it was awkward, and I didn't want to explain it to them, all of which was true. But what Joe didn't know, or frankly anyone for that matter, was the reason behind the breakup really stung. I didn't know how to tell him. He was the only guy I had ever dated who hadn't let me down.

I'd seen a guy in college who had an entirely different definition than I did of what it meant to be exclusive, and I ended up feeling like an idiot. So, there was that. Dating was a special kind of hell. I seemed to have a radar for guys who just wanted to get laid but who tried to pretend they wanted more. Five years ago, I'd dealt with a bout of cervical cancer. I'd had treatment and gone on to discover just a few months ago that I was infertile. The first guy I'd dated in years had dropped me completely when I told him that piece of news. Fuck it all.

I didn't want to tell Joe because even though he already had a child, maybe he wanted another one, and maybe it was a big deal.

Joe squeezed my hand, again prompting, "Stop fretting. We're going to enjoy this dessert, and that's all you're allowed to do."

I smiled over at him. "Okay." This moment was better than all the other moments I had to worry about, so I managed to forget it all. We enjoyed dessert, and I managed to kick my thoughts off that track until the universe laughed in my face. The guy who'd I'd almost let myself get serious with came walking in. He'd told me he thought he was falling for me. He'd told me that we'd figure it out, and then he'd ghosted me. When I'd run into him on the sidewalk months later, of all places, he'd said kids were really important to him. That encounter occurred the day before I decided to escape to Haven's Bay.

He was seated at a nearby table. It was impossible to miss the woman with him, who appeared to be pregnant. I didn't know how far along she was, but I was pretty sure it was further along than our breakup. Fuck my life. Joe saw me look over and nudged my knee with his under the table.

I looked back at him. Even though my devastation wasn't about the man sitting there, I knew I couldn't hide it. Joe knew me too well. This time, he didn't tell me not to fret.

Chapter Ten

JOE

I held Thea's hand firmly in mine as we walked out of the restaurant. Once we were walking outside with the Charles River glittering under the lights cast on the water, I paused and turned to face her.

"Who the hell was that, and what did he do?" I asked.

I'd seen the pain flash in her eyes back at the restaurant. Maybe he wasn't the source of all of her pain, but there was a story there, and she wasn't talking about it. I heard the swift intake of her breath before she lifted her eyes to mine.

"It wasn't him, Joe. You have to understand that part."

"Just tell me. I know you didn't tell me the whole story back at Christmas."

She blinked. "How did you know?"

"Because I know you, sweetheart. Maybe we hadn't seen each other in years, but call it emotional memory."

"Why didn't you say something then?" she pressed.

"Because we'd just seen each other for the first time in years and had an amazing night. I wasn't about to blow it by pushing you on an obviously sensitive topic. Tell me now."

She swallowed, looking out toward the river for a moment before bringing her gaze back to mine. "We dated for two months. I thought maybe we had something. It turned out to be a deal breaker that I can't have children. Except he lied and said it wasn't, and then he ghosted me. The woman with him looks pregnant." She shrugged. "I'm happy for them, but for her to be showing that much, I'm pretty sure they were seeing each other before he broke things off with me."

"I don't know if ghosting somebody is breaking things off. That's being a total coward as far as I'm concerned," I said flatly. Questions were swirling in my mind. "How do you know that was the deal breaker?"

"I ran into him on the sidewalk about two

months after he fell off the radar. I point-blank asked him what happened, and he said that was why." Thea took a breath, her throat working and a sheen of tears in her eyes. My heart twisted. "We haven't had this conversation, but I guess we should now. Like I told you before, I can't have children, so if that's a big deal for you, you should go home tonight."

"I'm not going home tonight."

The fact that her eyes widened and surprise flooded her gaze made me want to march back to that restaurant and punch that guy straight in the face.

"How do you know this won't be a thing for you?" she pressed.

"Because I know."

"Because you already have a son?"

"No, that's not it."

For the first time, I started to worry. Maybe it *was* a problem for her that I already had a son. Fuck. That was definitely something I couldn't undo, nor would I want to. I stepped closer, sliding an arm around her waist.

"Look at me," I pressed when her lashes swept down.

She took a shaky breath and lifted her eyes. "It's not that, okay? I love you. And part of loving somebody is going through the hard stuff together, whatever those things are. If you can't have kids, that's okay. Do you want kids? Because that kind of matters for you."

"I did," she said, her voice low.

"All right. So then, adoption."

"Really? It's that easy for you?"

I shrugged. "I don't know if it's that easy, but this isn't a deal breaker for me. That guy's a fucking asshole. Maybe I'm not an expert at life—"

"Joe, it's not that easy," Thea interjected, her voice low and insistent.

"I know it's not. I'm just saying. I look around at the world, and it's never easy. You know I had a brother who died when he was a baby. There are never any guarantees. Making a relationship about whether somebody can have kids is stupid."

Her forehead fell to my chest, and I felt her tremble as she took a deep breath.

"Okay." Her eyes glittered under the lights above us when she looked up.

"Can I go back and punch that guy?"

"He's not worth that. I think it just all collided. I found out I couldn't have kids, and then I told him. He said it was no big deal, and then he just fell off the face of the earth. You need to promise me that—" She pointed her index finger into my chest. "If we decide things aren't going to work out for us, you can't just stop talking to me."

"Sweetheart, you know I'd never do that. When your dad wouldn't let you take calls from me, I stuffed notes in your locker and called anyway. Until my dad told me I couldn't."

Her lips curled in a rueful smile. "I know. Can I say I'm sorry again about that?"

"You can, but you don't need to. I think we're well past that. It was high school. Shitty things happen, and as we've established, your dad was an asshole."

Her eyes had stopped glimmering with tears, and she laughed softly. "For real. He was."

"Can we go back to your place now?" I asked.

"Well, you're the one who stopped to talk, and it's kind of chilly out," she teased.

"It was me. Sorry about that." I dipped my head to steal a kiss before we began walking again.

"While we're on difficult subjects, how did you find out about...?" I paused, unsure how to clarify.

Because Thea knew me well, she finished for me. "About not being able to have children?" She glanced up at me as we walked. At my nod, she continued, "I had cervical cancer five years ago." I came to an abrupt stop on the sidewalk, a rush of fear slamming into my chest. "I'm fine and cancer-free," she added hurriedly. "Anyway, I had treatment, and it turns out it affected my fertility." She let out a sigh. "It is what it is."

My heart ached for her. It was obvious this hurt, and perhaps the hardest part was having the choice taken away. "I'm sorry," I said simply.

She squeezed my hand and turned to keep walking. "Thank you. I've adjusted to the information, even if I don't like it. Any other difficult questions you want to cover?" she asked, her tone light.

I sensed she didn't want to dwell on that. "What about your dad? Do you visit?"

"I have, but not often. My brothers have more feelings about it than I do."

"Yeah?"

"He was harder on them than me. My relationship with him was already stressed after what happened in high school. He was a jerk when we were growing up. He was verbally and emotionally abusive to everybody. So, I would never completely cut him out, but we won't be close. Our mom was the one who kept the family together anyway."

I glanced down at her. "That's kind of hard."

"It is. You have a nice family, so it's different."

"You're close with your brothers," I offered.

Her lips curled in a smile. "We are close. Maybe next Christmas we can do a big thing all together."

"Sounds like a plan. Now, let's get you home." I picked up the pace.

"You're kind of in a hurry."

"Well, you rushed us right out the door to dinner." I slid a hand down and gave her bottom a squeeze, savoring the way she squeaked.

Chapter Eleven

THEA

It was hard to decide what was best about being with Joe. There was the hot sex, which was *hot, hot, hot*, but then, there was waking up with him. Take now, for example. He was spooned behind me, and I could feel his arousal nestled against my bottom.

I was a little torn because I wanted to stay just like that and have him slide into me from behind, which he'd done many mornings on the weekends we'd spent together, but I also wanted to roll over and map his body with my lips. It was a toss-up.

This morning, I felt Joe come awake when he slid his palm over the curve of my belly and gave one of my breasts a lascivious squeeze. "Morning, sweetheart," he murmured against my neck, sending hot shivers chasing over my skin.

"Morning," I said, all breathy because he tended to steal my breath.

He rocked his arousal into my hips, and I pressed back because I couldn't resist. Another moment later, his hand slid down my belly and dipped into my curls. I was already wet, *really* wet, another state of being around Joe.

"Thea, you're all ready for me."

I couldn't help the gasp that escaped when his fingers delved into my folds. He sank two inside me. Before I could even savor that, he lifted my thigh as his fingers drew out. I felt the thick press of his crown before he filled me from behind and let out a ragged cry.

"Joe," I pleaded.

"Sweetheart. I'm already taking care of you," he teased as he nibbled on my neck and rocked his hips until he filled me deeply.

His fingers teased over my clit, and he fucked me slowly while the sun broke through the thin light of dawn, filtering through my windows. He thrust inside me, stretching me fully. My release was already building, small waves rolling onto the shore until a bigger one crashed and pleasure scattered through me in ripples. Joe thrust into me again, a slow pump, before he shuddered against me, my name coming out in a ragged shout.

He held me fast against him, dropping kisses on my neck as he brushed my tangled hair away from my face.

We lay like that for a while. It felt as if my entire body was smiling. The pleasure and joy of being with Joe went beyond sexual and sensual. He was like sunshine in my heart and soul. And I loved him.

I sobered for a minute when I remembered our conversation from last night. Because I was with Joe, I couldn't even dwell on things when he distracted me.

He squeezed my bottom and said, "Now, let me make you some coffee, and you can make me pancakes."

I giggled, and we rolled out of bed together before stumbling into the shower.

Chapter Twelve

THEA

"What?" Jane asked, her eyes going wide as she looked at me from across the table.

I took a bite of my sandwich, chewing quickly and hoping that would get rid of my embarrassment. I wasn't the kind of girl who did things on the sly or kept secrets, but I had been recently. At least, for over a month or so. She circled her hand in the air impatiently. We were at a small café we'd started coming to on occasion for lunch.

Sometimes, it was just Jane and me, and sometimes, Audrey and Sasha joined us. It felt like the four of us friends from high school were reconfiguring in Boston now, and I really liked it. But I digress.

I swallowed and dabbed at my mouth

with my napkin. "I went up to the house at Christmas, but you and Ian were there. I didn't want to mess up whatever was going on." Jane's cheeks flushed a little. I didn't mind her feeling a little disconcerted as well. "Remember how you bent your tire rim?"

Jane nodded. "Well, I did too, and Joe was the guy who responded. I didn't want to go to the house, and he offered to let me stay at his place." I knew my cheeks were fire engine red at this point because they were hot. I had to grab my napkin and use it as a fan. I even lifted my ice water and clasped it in my palms, willing my system to cool down.

My friend bit her lip, a sly grin unfurling when she released it. "Oh, wow. You and Joe." She reached over and squeezed my hand. "You were totally in love with him in high school. I think that's really sweet. You had to break up with him because your dad wouldn't even let you call him."

Emotion hit me in a rush. "I know. It was awful."

"How are things now?"

I took a deep breath. "Really good actually, like insanely good. We sort of picked up where we left off, except he's a lot better in bed."

Jane burst out laughing. "I think high

school probably isn't a good standard for anyone for that."

I laughed. "Definitely not."

Jane squeezed my hand again. Releasing it, she leaned back in her chair with a wide smile. "I'm so happy for you. So, is this a thing *thing*?"

"What's a thing *thing*?"

She rolled her eyes. "You know what I mean." She took a bite of her sandwich, chewing and swallowing before adding," Like are you guys really going to try to make this a relationship?"

"I want to. Emotionally, it's solid. But the problem is he lives in Haven's Bay, and I live here in Boston. Oh, and he has a son."

"Oh?" Audrey asked just as she arrived at the table. "Who has a son, and what do they have to do with you?"

"Joe," I replied.

"Joe Martinelli from high school?" Audrey sat down swiftly.

I took another bite of my sandwich, hoping Jane would explain for me because she was that kind of friend. She immediately did. "Well, apparently, when Ian and I were at the house in Haven's Bay, Thea was in Haven's Bay too. She and Joe reconnected, and they're hot and heavy again."

My friend Audrey—also my sister-in-law, happily married to my eldest brother, and they already had a baby—pressed her palm to her chest with a heartfelt sigh. "Oh, wow, I love that. It's perfect. I hated what happened to you two in high school. Joe was so good to you, totally sweet and into you, and you loved him."

"I really did."

"And now?"

"Um..." I started to hedge, but these were my friends, and they knew how much I'd loved Joe before. "I love him." Heat flared in my cheeks, but I couldn't keep from smiling.

Audrey glanced between Jane and me. "So when's the wedding?"

"What?" I squeaked.

"Oh, come on! You were totally in love before. You got back together secretly over the holidays, and you're in love all over again. Let's just plan a wedding."

"Um, I think that's a little early." I looked at Jane, who simply shrugged.

"Really? You've already gone through something hard. Is Joe upset about your dad keeping you from dating him back then?" Audrey asked.

"Not with me. He thinks my dad's an asshole."

"Well, he is," Audrey offered, and Jane nodded along. "Wait a sec. Christmas was over a month ago."

"I know, but I don't see you every weekend," I replied.

"No, but you've been keeping this a secret since then," Jane said pointedly.

"I know, it just felt..." I paused, unsure how to explain my feelings.

Audrey held my gaze before nodding. "It's private, something you wanted to keep special. I get it. I didn't want to tell people about Dallas right away either." At my nod, she continued, "So when's Joe coming down? We should plan a get-together for all of us." She circled her hand around the table.

"I've been going up to Maine more."

Jane chimed in, "And when's he coming down here?"

"He's been here, but with his son, we have to work around that schedule. It's going to be trial by fire with my brothers."

"No, it won't," Jane insisted. "None of them are like your dad."

"Thank god," I murmured.

"Does Sasha know?" Jane asked.

When I shook my head, she pulled her phone out. "I'm texting her right now."

I rolled my eyes. "Fine."

"Back to the wedding," Audrey interjected.

I looked over at her. "Joe lives in Haven's Bay, and he has a son. He's also running the family business there now. We're not at the wedding stage because him moving here isn't an option. I need to figure out if I can move and work up there."

Audrey drummed her fingertips on the table, and Jane chimed in. "Are you attached to Boston?"

"I like it. It's a great city."

"Can you imagine yourself living in Haven's Bay again?"

"Of course, I can. I grew up there," I said.

"What does he think?" Jane asked.

"He says he just wants to give us a chance. He doesn't want me to worry. He's pointed out I could commute to Boston. He's even offered to come here, but he's got a son, so I feel like that's not an option."

"I got sidetracked," Audrey commented. "How old is his son? What's the scoop there?"

"He had a one-night stand, and she got pregnant. I haven't even met his son yet. His name is Joey, he's six years old, and he looks just like Joe did when he was that age."

Jane angled her head to the side. "I think it makes sense to wait to meet his son."

Audrey nodded. "Dallas and I are very together, but if we weren't, I can't imagine just bringing someone into a child's world. It would need to be a sure thing. Anything else would be confusing."

"I'm in no rush. There's no pressure from me. I totally understand waiting. It's just a lot to think about."

"What ever happened with that guy Darren you were seeing last fall?" Audrey asked.

Fuckity, fuck, fuck.

"Yeah, I was. We broke it off."

Jane's perceptive gaze coasted over my face. "What's up?"

I internally sighed. "I found out I can't have children, and once I told him, he broke it off."

"Oh," Audrey breathed. "Are you okay?"

"I'd like the option, and it's not an option," I said flatly.

Audrey looked torn, and I reached over, sliding my arm around her shoulders and giving her a side hug. "I'll be fine. It's that thing no woman wants to talk about. You already had a baby, so obviously you can have kids. I don't know about Jane, but I'm assuming you haven't been told you can't have kids."

Jane shook her head. "Do you know what happened?"

"Cervical cancer. It was five years ago and not a big deal, but my doctor thinks the treatment affected my fertility."

"I'm sorry," Jane said softly.

I swallowed, surprised my emotions weren't getting the best of me. "Joe says it's fine, but that's why Darren broke things off."

Audrey's eyes narrowed. "What an asshole."

"We weren't that serious. I decided to tell him because we were allegedly exclusive. It turns out we weren't exclusive. I only found that out because Joe and I ran into him at a restaurant, and his girlfriend was pregnant. She's far enough along that there is no freaking way they weren't together before that."

"Oh, that asshole!" Jane exclaimed.

I shrugged. "I'm fine. It's just how he handled it. He ghosted me, which was weird and shitty."

"That is such a fucked-up thing to do, and it's really common," Audrey said, her nose scrunching up.

"I am fine, but I'm worried maybe Joe will change his mind later."

Jane gave me a long look. "Thea, don't make a problem where there isn't one. Look into adoption. There are options."

"I know, I know, but—"

"I think you're just throwing up a barricade," Audrey offered.

I pressed my lips together and let out a sharp sigh. "I don't think I am. And he has a son."

"So, you feel weird about that?" Jane prompted.

I took the last bite of my sandwich, hoping I could chew my emotions into oblivion.

My friends waited. I sipped water and glanced between them. "No, I'm not. It's just a lot."

"Maybe it would be a good idea to focus on what you and Joe have, which sounds pretty good," Audrey said gently.

"Apparently, he's great in bed," Jane offered with a sly smile.

My cheeks heated as I rolled my eyes.

"Well, that's always a win," Audrey chimed in.

"Don't you two dare tell me about your

sex lives! You're with my brothers," I muttered.

Audrey burst out laughing. "We'll just talk to each other about that."

Jane cast her a dubious glance. "Um, I don't want to hear about Ian's brother in bed."

I put my hands over my ears. "Can we stop the sex talk, please?"

My friends graciously let that topic go. By the time we parted, I did feel better. But the whole thing around children was niggling in the back of my thoughts. It really upset me that a part of me was bothered that Joe already had a child with someone else. It wasn't jealousy but a discomfort. I wanted a child with him, and that wasn't possible.

JOE

My son came barreling down the hallway with Dexter on his heels, his tail thumping against the wall as they rounded the corner into the living room.

"Hey, bud, slow down," I said, reaching over with an arm and catching him lightly by the shoulder.

Joey's dark hair was mussed, his eyes bright with his smile wide. Dexter circled us before crossing over and plunking down on the floor with a heartfelt sigh. Weekends with Joey ran Dexter ragged. They loved each other.

Joey flung himself on the floor beside Dexter, smiling over at me when he rolled his head to the side. "What's for dinner?" he asked.

"We're eating at Grammy and Gramps'. I'm sure it will be one of your favorites."

My son sat up and punched his arms into the air, letting out a whoop. "Grammy's a better cook than you, Dad."

"I know," I teased as I leaned over and ruffled his hair. "We need to be on time. Go wash your hands and face."

"My face?" Joey looked horrified at the thought.

"Yeah, you've got dirt on your cheek, and you need to brush your hair."

He slapped his hands to his head, smearing his hair down. "Is that good?"

"Joey." I patted him between the shoulder blades. "Get up, you know the drill. Go wash up. We're not leaving until you do."

He rolled his eyes. Yeah, at six years old, he rolled his eyes. His existence still blew my mind. He stood and trudged down the hallway. I heard the faucet running. I jogged into my bedroom and sped through a shower. I'd had a busy day and even done some work in the garage, so I had to scrub my nails. My mind spun to my planned conversation this evening. My parents knew I was dating Thea, but they didn't know I planned to ask her to marry me. We hadn't figured out who was going to live where yet, but I wasn't going to let this chance pass by.

I loved her. I'd loved her in high school. When she'd moved away after high school, I'd figured that was the answer to my questions about our future. We'd been dating for four months now, and I'd seen her as much as I could. The only times I didn't see her was when Joey was with me. She was still nervous about meeting him, but I thought it was time. I needed to let my parents know my plans. Once they knew, I intended to finally introduce Joey to her.

I was nervous. My mom was still pissed off at Thea's dad about what happened in high school. My mom was also super cautious, all because Joey was the product of a one-night stand. It seemed my dick didn't have the best—shall we say?—judgment. Joey's mom, Vanessa, was not the most stable woman, and I stressed about that on occasion.

My mom wanted me to fight for full custody, but I didn't know if that was best. Joey's mom loved him and did her best. I thought that was the best anybody could ask for from parents. I loved my parents, and they were solid, but Lord knows, they weren't perfect. My dad was on the strict side, and my parents were known for emotional arguments. We were a loving, loud, boisterous type of family.

I toweled my hair dry and took a last look in the mirror before zipping down the hallway. My son was standing in the bathroom, looking at himself solemnly in the mirror. He had actually brushed his hair. The part was crooked, but I didn't give a shit how he parted his hair. I could tell he'd washed his face because his cheeks were pink. When he looked over at me, his freckles stood out a little.

"How do I look, Dad?"

I dipped my chin. "You look great. Grammy is going to give you a thumbs-up."

Joey sighed. "No, she's gonna give me a big kiss on my cheek, and it's gonna squeak."

I chuckled, resting my hand between his shoulders as we walked out of the bathroom. "She loves you."

"I know. I love her too."

After I started driving, he startled the hell out of me. "Mom says you have a girlfriend."

I took a breath before taking a quick

glance in the rear view mirror. He didn't look upset but rather curious and waiting expectantly. "I do. What did your mom have to say about that?"

"Just that you have a girlfriend."

"I was planning to talk to you about her soon. How do you feel about that?"

"I don't know," he replied, fidgeting with the zipper tab on his jacket.

"Good answer. You haven't even met her yet, so it's hard to know how you might feel."

"I know. I can't have an opinion until I know someone. It's not fair. That's what you said about that kid who moved to town that I didn't like."

"Brandon?" I prompted.

"Uh-huh."

"You're friends with him now, right?"

"I am." Joey met my gaze asI glanced back when I stopped at an intersection. "What's her name?"

"Thea."

"How do you spell that?" He loved knowing how to spell words and names.

"T-h-e-a."

He silently mouthed her name. "Thea," he repeated back to me. "I've never known anyone with that name."

"She's the only Thea I know too."

"When do I get to meet her?"

Sometimes, I thought my son was telepathic. "I was planning to talk to your grandparents about her tonight. She means a lot to me."

"But it's not been very long," he chimed in.

"How do you know it hasn't been very long?" I returned, casting him a quick grin.

"Because I haven't met her yet. You always told me if you brought someone into our family, it would be someone you knew for a while."

"Thanks for listening. I've actually known her since I was your age."

"What?!" he exclaimed, slapping both palms on his knees. "No way."

"Way. She's from Haven's Bay. We grew up together. She was my girlfriend in high school. I was in love with her."

When I slid my eyes to the back seat, Joey's face held a look of horror. "You were in love with a girl in school?"

I chuckled at the distaste in his tone. "I was. When you get older, you might like girls."

He cast me a skeptical look. "Um, okay." After a pause, he continued, "So, you've known her since, since... before I was born."

When this dawned on him, his eyes went wide, and he looked over at me. "I have. I'm going to talk to Grammy and Gramps about her tonight. I thought maybe she could come up for the weekend the next time you're staying with me."

My son looked out the window. His little shoulders lifted as he took in a deep breath before letting it out in a giant gust.

"What was that?" I asked.

"A brave breath."

"What's a brave breath?"

"We learned about it in school. It's something you do when you're not sure about something or worried and maybe your tummy hurts. You take a deep breath, and you feel brave," he explained.

"Are you worried about meeting her? I understand if you are."

"I want you to have a girlfriend."

"Yeah?"

"Uh-huh." I stole a quick glance, and he'd turned to look out the window again. And then, kicking my heart like it was a can to the side of the road, he added, "I wish Mom was your girlfriend."

Oh, fuck. Every once in a very long while, maybe three times in his entire life, Joey said something like this. My heart ached every time.

"Yeah?" I asked.

Aside from the one night that resulted in Joey's existence, we'd never been together. He didn't have memories of us being together.

"Yeah, then we'd be like a regular family."

I gathered my thoughts. "Joey, we've talked about this before. There are all kinds of families. There is no regular family." When Joey was younger, I'd actually met with a therapist because I'd wanted guidance about how to talk to him about this. "Families come in all shapes and sizes. Regular is whatever shape a family is. Mom's a part of our family, but she doesn't live with us. Grammy and Gramps are a part of our family too, but they also don't live with us."

He took another brave breath and looked back at me. "I know. Maybe you can be with Thea, and we could do fun stuff together."

"I'm definitely with Thea, and I would like it if we did fun stuff together."

His hair bounced with his nod. "Should I tell Grammy about her?"

"Nope. I'll handle it."

My little boy looked over at me, his brows almost sitting at his hairline with curiosity. "What if I want to tell her first?"

Oh, fuck my life. I didn't say that thought out loud, though. "You know what? That's fine. Why don't you tell her about this conversation?"

"Okay."

Chapter Fourteen

JOE

My mother took a sip of her coffee, some discount brand straight from the can. That was her favorite kind of coffee. Whatever the best deal was.

"I don't know, Joey."

She still called me Joey, and she called my son Joey Jr. He was currently sound asleep in the living room in my dad's recliner. She'd made his favorite spaghetti casserole for dinner. He had, in fact, told her about our conversation on the drive over here.

"I don't trust Thea's father," my mother added.

"Well, I don't think Thea trusts her father either. You know that what happened hurt her as much as me."

"I know, but I didn't like the way her father treated our family like we were less than," she said pointedly.

"Thea never felt that way, and her family doesn't think we're less than anyone now. I know her mom passed away, but she never thought that about us."

My mother smoothed a hand over her mostly silver hair, which was twisted into a braid that hung down her back. She let out a soft sigh, eyeing me cautiously. "You love her, and you plan to marry her. After only four months."

My father, bless his blunt-speaking self, peered over his newspaper, offering, "Hon, I asked you to marry me after one month, and all I'd gotten was a kiss on the porch."

He grinned at me and winked before folding his paper back up and continuing to read. My mother's cheeks flushed slightly. "I know, but—"

I cut in, "Mom, it's not like we've just met each other. We've known each other since we were kids.

"Is she going to move up here?"

"We haven't figured that out. All that matters to me is that I love her, I want to marry her, and I want to introduce her to Joey. The rest we can figure out."

"But—" she began again.

"Mom, please. You're a big part of my life. You and Dad. I know I don't have all the answers, but I have the most important one."

"What's that?"

"I love her, and she loves me."

My mother's eyes teared up, and she smiled softly. "You always were a softie. You were so brokenhearted in high school when her dad wouldn't let her see you anymore. I just don't understand how come you didn't fall for Joey's mom like this."

"Oh my god, Mom. We've been over this. I met Vanessa at a bar. It was a hookup."

My mom gasped, her hand flying to her chest, showing some faux outrage, in my opinion. Meanwhile, my dad chuckled.

"I like Vanessa as a friend, but we're not going to be together like that. I can't believe you're saying that when lately you've been trying to get me to fight for full custody."

My mom sighed. "You're right. I'm not being reasonable. Are you going to bring Thea to see us soon?"

"It depends on if you're going to be nice to her," I said pointedly, taking a swallow of the so-so coffee.

"Your mother will be nice to Thea. She's

just going to worry. You were pretty heart-broken before," my dad interjected.

"I know, and I understand."

"Isn't she some bigwig lawyer in Boston?" my mother asked.

"She works for a law firm there. She has a small apartment that probably costs a fortune."

My mother clucked. "Exactly. What if she wants to stay there?"

"Fine with me. People commute all the time. We'll figure it out. She's too important to me to let geography get in the way."

My mother drained her coffee and gave me an assessing look. "You find out what she likes, and I'll make dinner for her."

"I will, Mom. Thank you." I stood and pressed a kiss to her cheek.

Chapter Fifteen

THEA

Staring at myself in the mirror, I grabbed my brush again and ran it through my hair. I had mostly straight hair, but there was just enough wave that it sometimes curled in weird angles. For example, right now.

It was flattening against the side of my forehead and then winging out. I dampened the brush and ran it through the wave just as Joe appeared. "Are you ready?"

He must have seen the frustration in my eyes. He stepped behind me in the mirror, sliding his hands around my waist and resting his chin on my shoulder. "You look beautiful. Why is your hair wet on one side?"

He dropped a kiss on the side of my neck. Even though I was unsettled and stressed about how I looked, that subtle touch sent a shiver through my body. Because it was Joe, and it was me, and that was how it was with us.

"It's got this weird wave," I said, gesturing to the offending spot in my hair.

Joe straightened and eyed my hair quizzically in the mirror. "I don't notice anything," he finally said.

I rolled my eyes. "Of course, you wouldn't."

"Joey's not going to notice your hair, like, at all, and neither are my parents."

I took a shaky breath. "I know, but—"

"Sweetheart." He turned me around by the shoulders. "Stop looking in the mirror."

I peered up at him and took another shallow breath. "I'm nervous."

"Really? I didn't notice," he said, his lips curling at the corners.

"Joe." I nudged him lightly with my elbow, right in his hard abs.

His gaze was understanding as he looked at me. "It's fine. I understand why you're nervous. I really do. My son might notice a number of things, but your hair is probably on the bottom of the list. Now, come on. We need to go pick him up."

"Should I wait here?" I asked as he caught

my hand in his and tugged me out of the bathroom.

Before we reached the door to his bedroom, he turned. "Yes, I always pick him up."

"Should I wait here?" I repeated.

"No, I think you should go with me. I told Joey you'd be with me, and cars are very forgiving when it comes to chatting with kids."

With his hand curled around mine, he led me down the hallway behind him. I went with a little resistance.

"What do you mean cars are very forgiving?"

"Because there's not as much eye contact. It's a small trick I thought I figured out myself. When I told my mom, she laughed because she already knew." He rolled his eyes as he dropped my hand when we reached the kitchen.

He opened a drawer by the doorway into the garage, where he kept his keys and various sundry items. "They don't have to look at you. Whenever he's in trouble for something, even if it's minor, it's the perfect place to chat. I manufacture an errand, not like it's hard because my list of things to do is endless. That's when we talk. You'll be in the front seat. He'll be buckled up in the back asking tons of questions."

"Sweetheart, I know you're freaking out, but it'll be okay. Now, we're going to be late if we don't go."

I reluctantly followed Joe into the garage and climbed into the passenger seat of his SUV. I laced my fingers tightly together in my lap and tried to quell the anxiety rising in wave after wave inside me.

Joe's son was the most important person in his entire life, and I was about to meet him. This was so fucking stressful, and I didn't want to freak out. I had no idea how Joey's mom felt about my presence in Joe's life.

Before I could think better of it, I blurted out my question. "Does Joey's mom know I'll be there for the pickup?"

"Yep, already told her." Joe paused as he tapped the button to close the garage door after he backed out. "She knows we've been seeing each other for months, and she knows that we dated in high school."

"Do you two usually talk ahead like this?"

"I actually saw a therapist to help me figure out how to handle the whole co-parenting thing. She said we should have conversations about all important matters, even if we couldn't get along. Honestly, we mostly get along. We're not close. I know that sounds weird, but it is what it is. From the few other people I know who have to deal with custody stuff, I think it's probably better that we didn't have a relationship before. There're no hard feelings about stuff."

I had so many questions about Joey's mom, but now definitely wasn't the time. "Where do you pick him up?"

"The school bus drops him off at the garage. We used to do house drop-offs, but Joey would always try to get one of us to stay and hang out, and that's really not what I want. This keeps it clean."

Oh. So many questions crowded my thoughts. I took another nervous breath as we reached downtown Haven's Bay because that meant we were almost there. The main location for his garage was just past the downtown area.

He reached over, sliding his hand between mine, effectively unlacing my fingers. His touch was warm and reassuring, and my anxiety instantly let up inside. He came to a stop at a corner, and I glanced over to find his gaze waiting for me.

"It's going to be fine."

"What if he doesn't like me?"

"He's six years old. He likes most everybody. You're the first woman I've brought to meet him, and he knows you mean a lot to me."

I swallowed and took a breath because I couldn't decide if that made matters better or worse. Joe simply held my hand and kept driving. Before I knew it, we were turning in at the garage.

He gave my hand one last squeeze before he parked and turned off the engine. I wasn't sure what to do. We hadn't discussed if I should get out of the SUV or wait here. Fortunately, I didn't have to dwell long.

"Come on in. Joey will be hanging out along the edges of the garage where he's allowed. He'll be distracted and happy."

"Are you sure I should come in?"

At his nod, I climbed out. Before we even got to the glass door that led into the back of the garage, I heard the sound of footsteps approaching, then a little boy burst out of the door.

"Dad!" he called.

He bumped into Joe's legs as Joe released my hand and leaned down to swing him up into his arms.

"Hey, big guy." He lifted him before setting him against his hip.

Joe's son turned to look at me. He looked so much like Joe had when we were in elementary school together that my heart lodged into my throat and emotion roared through me. Oh, wow. He was a miniature version of Joe.

"Hi," Joey said, completely calm.

"Hi, I'm Thea."

He wiggled, and Joe set him on the ground. "I'm Joey," he announced as he took several steps to stand in front of me, holding his hand out formally.

I shook his hand, and he held it as he studied my face. "My dad loves you."

"Oh, well, I know he loves you very much," I returned.

"Of course, he does," Joey replied matter-of-factly, so utterly confident in his father's love for him that my heart twisted in my chest.

I couldn't help the little laugh that slipped out. "Of course."

"He's my dad. He's known you a lot longer than me, though."

"That's true," I agreed. "He's known me since kindergarten, at least."

"Maybe before that. I think our parents might have occasionally gone to the same church," Joe offered.

Another nervous laugh bubbled out. "It's very nice to meet you, Joey."

A big smile broke across his face. "You too." He held his hand up for what I assumed was a high five. I didn't hesitate and slapped my palm to his. "I like you," he announced.

"You do?"

"Well, so far. You're pretty," Joey offered.

Joey clambered into the SUV, sighing as Joe checked to make sure he was buckled into the booster seat. Although I'd known he was a father since he'd told me, all of a sudden, it became real. Before this moment, it had been an idea in my brain. Now, the knowledge was concrete, and he gave off major dad energy. I thought it was sexy. Not that I needed anything to make Joe seem sexier to me. His easy confidence and protectiveness were just hot.

I climbed into the front passenger seat and promptly discovered why Joe said car rides were easy with kids. If you could deal with the conversation, that is. Joey talked almost nonstop. He wasn't even focused on me. He talked about school, about some girl who he thought was annoying, his favorite class, and then his most hated class. It was a lot. I just listened. A few times Joe caught my eyes and grinned.

I quietly took a breath and let it out, finally starting to relax. It was all going great until Joey tapped me on the shoulder, focusing his piercing gaze on me when I glanced back. "When are you and Dad getting married? Grammy said Dad's asking you."

Chapter Sixteen

JOE

Oh, hell. Fuck my life. I wanted to think my mom would have been sensible enough not to mention to Joey that I wanted to marry Thea. Sometimes, my mom said too much, especially when it came to me.

I caught Thea's expression and winced slightly. She was startled all right, but she handled it like a pro.

"Well, I don't know. Maybe we don't need to worry about that right now."

"If Dad's in love with you, I want you to get married," my son replied, his gaze swinging to me in the rearview mirror.

"How about we pump the brakes on this?" I commented.

"Does that mean to slow down?" Joey asked.

Like most kids his age, Joey tended to think literally.

"Yeah, slow down. We're not to marriage yet. I love Thea, and that's what's important right now. We'll figure the rest out when the time is right."

I was seriously winging this and hoped he hadn't just screwed things up with Thea.

Joey shrugged. "All right. I guess you can just be in love."

I couldn't help but chuckle and was relieved to hear Thea's soft laughter beside me.

"What's for dinner tonight?" Joey asked, blessedly moving on.

"We're going out."

Joey sat up straighter. "Where?"

"What do you think about Pizza Play?"

"Yes!" Joey exclaimed, punching one fist and then the other into the air. He wiggled sideways in his seat, entirely distracted from the wedding idea. "It's my favorite pizza place, and they have a playground. Can we go now?"

I glanced at the dashboard clock, having already anticipated this. "That's the plan."

Thea knew where we were going already. This pizza place was a rarity in the universe of pizza and parenting. They had gourmet wood-fired pizza, but it was also totally family friendly with an indoor play area on one side. For parents, it was heaven with delicious pizza, a kid-friendly menu, and occupied children.

With Joey practically bouncing in his seat all the way to the pizza place, it didn't take much effort to keep him talking. He was full of information for Thea. He told her about the kids in his class, his favorite gym teacher, his favorite substitute teacher, and his favorite lunch menu, which was called the fun stuff menu, and they only had it once per quarter.

"What's the fun stuff menu?" Thea asked.

His eyes went wide as he spun in his seat. I called over my shoulder. "Stay in your seat belt."

"Okay," he said quickly. "Did you guys have the fun stuff menu when you were in school? Dad said you went to elementary school together."

Thea smiled. "We did. And we didn't have the fun stuff menu. What's on that menu?"

"It's tater tots with cheese and grilled cheese sandwiches and pizza and hot dogs and milkshakes," Joey explained.

I caught Thea's eyes, commenting,

"That's basically what our regular menu was, if I recall."

Joey's mouth dropped open as he looked between us. I winced slightly. "Sorry, they feed you much healthier food now."

"That's not fair," he said slowly.

"It probably is. I think you're going to be a lot healthier when you grow up than I am."

"You eat healthy now," he protested.

I thought I heard a snort come from Thea, but Joey was too distracted to notice. I did eat mostly healthy now, but it was because I had a son and needed to try to make sure he had healthy food. Left to my own devices, without anyone else to be responsible for, I ate mostly takeout, which wasn't all bad, but fast food was fast and convenient, not necessarily healthy. The nights when I covered the emergency service calls, I got by on coffee, doughnuts, and the occasional fast food burger. It was what it was.

"I'm asking the principal how come we can't eat the way you guys used to eat," Joey announced.

"She's not going to go for it," I replied.

"How do you know?" he protested.

"I just know. Count your blessings that you have the fun stuff menu once a quarter."

Joey let out an elaborate sigh.

"You'll be all right," I promised.

The rest of the drive passed by in a blink.

"When did this place open?" Thea asked as we were crossing the parking lot.

I wanted to reach for her hand as I replied, "A few years ago."

Even though Joey knew she meant something to me, I hesitated until he glanced accusingly between us. "Why aren't you holding her hand?"

I could tell Thea was trying not to laugh because the corners of her mouth pinched together. I reached for her hand immediately. "I am now."

"Wow, Dad. You don't even know how to be a good boyfriend."

"I don't?" I pressed while Thea's shoulders shook with laughter.

He shook his head and glanced at Thea. "I'll have to explain it to him."

Once again, she succeeded at not laughing out loud. "I can't wait," she said solemnly.

A few minutes later, we were waiting in line, and Thea's eyes were scanning the chalkboard menu mounted behind the counter. "Which side are we sitting on?" Joey asked.

I looked down at him, puzzled. "The side

with the play area." This had never been something he wondered about.

"Yeah, but this is a date," he replied.

"What do you mean?" I asked.

"You're taking Thea out to dinner," he replied, his tone exasperated.

"I'd love to sit over near the play area," Thea chimed in. "Don't you want to?" Thea squatted, rocking on her heels and bringing her eyes level with Joey's.

Joey looked from her to me and back again before he nodded sagely. "Ah, that'll give you some private time. Okay, we'll sit on the playground side."

Thea smiled. "Okay, but if you want us to sit at a regular table, that's fine too."

"Nope." Joey was resolute in this. He seemed to be taking his wingman responsibilities seriously.

After we ordered and got seated, he looked from me to Thea again, narrowing his eyes almost comically. "Well, Dad, here's what I know about having a girlfriend."

I leaned one elbow on the table and reached with my other hand for Thea's underneath, giving it a squeeze as I laced my fingers with hers. She looked at him attentively, her expression very serious.

"I can't wait," I offered.

With a solemn nod, my son began. "Well, you should be writing her a note once a day." He looked toward Thea. "Is he doing that?"

"Do texts count?" she asked.

Joey was thrown by this. "I'm not sure. I don't have my own cell phone. I write them on paper and fold them up." His nose scrunched as he contemplated. "But when you're in Boston, that's not easy."

"Okay, and then what?" I asked.

"You need to hold her hand at lunch. I don't get to eat dinner with my girlfriend, but I'm pretty sure that would be one of the rules."

"Joey, who's your girlfriend?" I felt pressed to ask.

"Jamie."

"Oh, how long has she been your girlfriend?"

"A week. My girlfriend last month was Tara."

"Oh, I didn't know that." I was a little thrown by these details. It was only weeks ago when he was horrified at the idea of liking any girl.

Joey shrugged casually as he lifted his chin. "I don't tell you everything, Dad."

Thea squeezed my hand.

"Also, no kissing on the lips. You can only

kiss her on the cheek, and only once. I haven't had a girlfriend for Valentine's Day, but Tara told me guys have to plan for a card and some candy. Like those little heart things, the ones I don't like." He scrunched his nose at this.

"All of that sounds great. I appreciate your advice," I said.

"If you need to run the notes by me when Thea's here, just ask. I check on three of my friends' notes at school to make sure they're nice."

"What is nice?" Thea asked.

"Just the handwriting. Mine's pretty good. You know I got an A in handwriting." He looked over at me.

"You sure did." It was a miracle I didn't laugh. I did have to squeeze Thea's hand really hard to let that energy out somewhere.

Another bonus about this place was they were pretty quick with the food. Our pizza arrived, and Joey was immediately absorbed in eating. After he scarfed down two slices of his beloved extra pepperoni and extra cheese pizza, he dashed off to the play area. Thea paused between bites to smile over at me, a sly glint in her eyes.

"You need to up your game. Handwritten notes and so on."

"I can handle that." I leaned over and stole a kiss.

I meant for it to be quick, but it was Thea and me, and the second my lips met hers, the fire ignited. Before I knew it, I was sliding my hand into her hair and sweeping my tongue into her mouth. She made an inarticulate sound in the back of her throat and then pressed her palm to my chest. I drew back, gratified to see the pink flush staining her cheeks.

"Joe," she scolded in a whisper.

"What? It's just a kiss. Joey didn't even see, plus you're spending the weekend with us at the house."

"I know. We didn't talk about the details. Should I sleep on the couch?"

"No," I said firmly. "He already knows I love you, and, apparently, he's ready to plan the wedding."

Thea giggled, and I leaned back, actually forcing myself to take another bite from my pizza slice just so I didn't kiss her again.

"He looks just like you," she said, her tone almost wondering.

"So I'm told."

"It's kind of a trip. I remember you when you were that age. You never wanted to be my boyfriend back then."

"I don't think I had a single girlfriend in elementary school and not even middle school. That really wasn't my thing. I think my son is sweeter than I was back then."

"You were a really great boyfriend in high school," she said, her tone sincere as her eyes held mine.

"I tried. It wasn't hard with you."

Her brows rose in question. "You were my one and only serious girlfriend. Honestly, you're my only serious girlfriend."

"You weren't serious with Joe's mom?"

"Thea, I already told you. It was a one-night stand. I'm not proud of that, but that's what it was. I think we handle co-parenting well, but there's nothing romantic there, as far as the relationship goes." I could tell she was worrying. I leaned over, stealing another kiss. "You need to remember to stop worrying."

"What do you think I'm worrying about?" she asked when I lifted my lips from hers.

"I know that look. You're worrying."

A rueful smile curled her lips, and she took another bite of pizza. "Do I need to be worried about your parents tomorrow night?"

Chapter Seventeen

THEA

"Absolutely not," Joe said with more confidence than I expected.

"How can you be so sure?" I pressed

"My parents loved you before, and they'll love you again."

"Yeah, but my dad made us break up, and they probably didn't appreciate how he treated you."

He shrugged. "They're adult enough to be able to make the distinction between you and your father. Plus, my mom's the one who told Joey I wanted to marry you."

"You really told your mom that?" I squeaked.

"Sure, I did. I want to marry you, so it's nothing but the truth." He was all easy breezy about it. "Thea, you're it for me. I don't care what I have to do to help you believe me, but you are."

My eyes stung with a rush of hot tears, and my heart felt as if it was about to be yanked out of my chest, the way a kite billowed abruptly when a gust of wind caught it. The sensation was joyful and terrifying because I couldn't control it.

"Oh, oh, oh, wow," I breathed.

The sound of kids laughing in the play area reached us with the pitter-patter of feet following as a pair of girls ran by squealing. "I know this isn't a romantic place," Joe said, his lips curling in a rueful smile. "I should have taken Joey's advice and sat on the other side."

Joy rose definitively through the rush of panic and emotion. I reached for his hand where it rested on the table, grabbing on to it as if it were a lifeline. His hand curled around mine, his touch strong and warm and sure. "This is perfect." His intent gaze held mine while my heart thudded.

"Yeah?" His low, gravelly voice sent a shiver skating over my skin.

"It means a lot that you wanted me to meet Joey. You've really never introduced anyone to him before?"

Joe shook his head swiftly. "My life has

been busy, and it's..." He paused, reaching to take a swallow of his water with his free hand. After he set it down, he angled to face me. "I'm busy with work and with my son. I wasn't against having a relationship, but nobody came along. I never stopped wondering about you even though I kind of thought it was a lost cause."

His comments stung. The memory hurt, like a jagged scrape torn open again.

The squeeze of his hand around mine brought my focus back. "Then I saw you, and it all just felt right. I don't even have to think about it."

"But—"

He placed two fingers over my lips. "Let me say this, and I'm going to keep reminding you as long as I need to. All the hard parts that other people struggle with come easy for us. Geography is the only detail we have to figure out. In the big scheme of things, that's not much. Boston's not that far away."

"Okay." I took a breath, the tension in my chest easing.

Joy mingled with the intense love I felt for this man.

I heard Joey calling, "Dad, Thea, look!"

We swiveled in unison to see him standing atop the slide. "Watch me."

Joe squeezed my hand, and we watched as Joey slid down the slide in a rush, bouncing on the ballooned landing platform at the bottom.

———

Joe was slick. He'd told me about our plans for dinner, but I didn't realize his other motives. Joey was *completely* wiped out as soon as we got home. He said he wanted to watch TV, but he fell asleep on the couch about five minutes into his favorite show. Joe held a finger to his lips as he scooped him into his arms and took him to bed. He'd already made sure Joey brushed his teeth.

"It's not even eight o'clock," I commented when he returned to the living room.

He winked as he slipped onto the couch beside me. "Trust me, he won't wake up. That's one thing kids have good."

"What?"

"Sleeping straight through the night. It's crazy. Once he falls asleep, Joey is *out* until morning comes. Once he wakes up, he's like a cricket bouncing around."

I giggled. "Nice description."

"Hey, trust me. Wait until you see him. We won't be sleeping in tomorrow."

"Should we go to bed early then?"

Joe dusted a kiss on my neck in that sensitive spot right behind my ear, and I shivered all over. "Yes, we should."

He lifted the remote and clicked off the TV. I stood and started to move away, but he caught me by the hand. Spinning toward him, I found myself caught in the beam of his gaze. My face was just above his as I stood over where he was seated on the couch.

He leaned forward, palming my cheek. "It's good to have you here," he murmured in a gruff whisper.

"It's good to be here," I whispered in return, my forehead falling to his.

He kissed me—slow, lazy, and deep. By the time he lifted his lips from mine, my knees were liquid, and I was gasping for air. I melted straight through, like a stick of butter in the hot sun.

"Joe," I scolded. "We're in the living room."

He threw me an unabashed grin. "I know. We're gonna go to the bedroom just in case Joey wakes up, but the odds of him waking up and walking out here after a night like tonight are probably less than zero."

He stood and lifted me into his arms. There was something delicious about being carried by a strong man. I breathed in his scent—crisp with that hint of the ocean that always seemed to cling to him. I pressed kisses on the inside of his neck, murmuring, "You smell good."

"Slow down, sweetheart. We've got to get to the bedroom," he rasped before pausing to kiss me thoroughly.

He moved like a cat, stealthy and silent, down the hallway. Once we were in his bedroom, He eased me down and closed the door. "I'm not locking it," he said. "It's a dad thing."

"Makes sense. If he needs to come in, you don't want him locked out."

"Exactly. We're gonna be under the covers and everything."

"We are?" I teased. "Oh, I like this. It feels like we're breaking a rule."

Joe's chuckle was low and sent a shiver chasing through me. In a hot second, he was tugging my clothes off while I yanked at his. We fell onto the bed, and he rolled over to lay a deep kiss on me. When we broke apart to gasp for air, he rolled me with him and pulled the covers over both of us.

"Have we done it under the covers?" I asked.

He nipped at my neck. "Not recently. I

remember we fooled around once or twice at my parents under the covers back in the day."

"Oh, wow. Now that's a memory."

"Here's another one." I felt the motion of his lips on my collarbone. The feel of his calloused palm sliding up the inside of my thigh sent sparks in a scatter over my skin. He pushed my knee to the side before he disappeared under the covers. His lips dropped kisses on my belly, and his fingers delved into my channel.

I was already slippery wet with arousal, and I let out a gasp, immediately yanking the sheets to my mouth. It was all I could do not to cry out when I felt his mouth join the fun. Joe knew his way around, driving me crazy. He teased me to the edge of madness, making love to me with his fingers and his mouth. Again and again and again, he just barely glanced over my swollen and needy clit with his tongue.

He ignored my muffled pleas. Finally, *finally*, he rose, resting his hips in the cradle of mine. His thick arousal slid through my folds. I tasted myself on him when he kissed me.

He drew back, murmuring, "I want to feel you come on my cock, sweetheart."

Then I felt the delicious intoxicating stretch as he sank into me in a slow thrust.

My orgasm was already threatening. He pulled back, giving another slow pump before I shattered, my orgasm pulling me under like a riptide. As I came in deep surges, he kissed me, capturing my cries in his mouth. I felt the heat of his release filling me as he shuddered roughly, burying his mouth against my neck in a hot, open-mouthed kiss.

He rolled swiftly away, bringing me with him, and I rested against his muscled body. My heartbeat echoed through my body, a rolling drum of emotion and sated need.

This. It always felt so profoundly right, with Joe, right in a way it hadn't felt before, even during the heady days of our forbidden crush so many years ago. I let my fingertips trail over his chest before lifting my head and resting my chin on my palm, directly over his heart. He opened his eyes to meet mine, a barely-there grin curling the corners of his mouth.

"What?" he prompted.

Leaning forward, I dropped a kiss in the divot at the base of his throat before lifting my head and replying, "I don't know. It's really good to be here."

"It's really good for you to be here." His fingers slid through my hair and down my back.

"Are you up early on the weekends usually when Joey's here?"

Joe's laugh was dry. "I don't have much choice. Let's just say I'm grateful getting up early comes naturally. He's conked out now, but trust me, he'll be bouncing around in the morning. I usually try to beat him up."

I giggled, and he rolled his eyes. "You know what I mean."

"I know what you mean. You mean beat him to being awake."

"Precisely. What's the plan for tomorrow?"

Chapter Eighteen

THEA

Breakfast with Joey and Joe was the easy part of my day. By the time evening rolled around, my nerves were twisted into knots. I knew Joe's parents. They were nice people, and I liked them. But I hadn't forgotten the disapproving glances I'd gotten from them after my father told me I couldn't see Joe anymore in high school.

They were an emotional, loving family. I remembered thinking they'd probably wished I'd had more nerve. I didn't know how to stand up to my father back then. It had seemed impossible.

In the last few years or so since my brothers and I had started coming back to Haven's Bay for vacations and holidays, I'd seen them a few times around town. Maybe it was all in my mind, but I was still convinced they held it against me.

Joe kept reassuring me. "Thea, it's fine. Stop worrying."

He was standing behind me in the mirror in the bathroom as I smoothed my hand over my hair. "Easy for you to say. They adore you. You're their son. I'm the one who broke your heart."

"*You* didn't break my heart." His hands came to my shoulders, giving a light squeeze before they slid down my arms. "My heart was broken, but I didn't blame you. I blamed your dad because he was an asshole. Plus, who knows how it would have turned out if we had tried to stay together when we were that young? Most couples don't make it when it starts that young."

I turned, resting my hips against the counter. He lifted one of my hands, turning it over and dropping a kiss in the center of my palm. Ripples of warmth radiated from that touch, reverberating through my system. "I know, but—"

He interjected. "Sweetheart, we can't change the past. We're back together, and that's all that matters. We're older and wiser, and that's probably for the best. Last night and today went great with Joey."

I took a quick breath, letting it out in a gust. "I know it did. He's really awesome."

Joe shrugged. "He is awesome, but he's being very well-behaved this weekend. Trust me, when he gets comfortable with you, he won't always be the angel he's being this weekend."

I laughed. "No?"

"He's pretty good, but he's like any kid. He's never perfect. When he's got energy to burn, it can be tough." He dipped his head and dropped a quick kiss on my mouth. "Let's go. You've got this. My parents loved you before, and they'll love you again."

He'd said some variation of that a number of times. I took a shaky breath. "Okay."

"Dear, you look lovely," Maria said.

I managed to smile in return, although the butterflies in my belly were not the good kind. Right now, they felt like rats scurrying about instead of the pleasant nervous sensation I got whenever Joe gave me a look.

"Thank you. It's really good to see you

again." I looked over toward Joe's dad, making sure to encompass him in my smile.

"Have a seat. I've already got dinner ready. It's Joey Jr's favorite, and Joey said you would like it." She gestured to the table. "It's a spaghetti meatball casserole. He likes when I cook it in a pan, so he can slice it," she offered with a little chuckle as she glanced through the archway to Joey, who was in the living room currently watching a cartoon on the television.

"It looks like some work is happening on your family's home," Joe's father, John, commented.

I sat down at the table, and Joe sat beside me, sliding his palm onto my thigh under the table and giving my knee a reassuring squeeze. I tried to ignore his touch although it did feel good.

"Yep. We've been slowly getting everything taken care of. My brother Ian is replacing all the windows and sills, which is a lot of work," I explained.

John arched his brows and nodded. "Those windows are ancient, not specifically on your house, but on any of those older houses. That's why I told Joe here it was smart to build new. He didn't buy an old house, just got the property and built a new place."

"Definitely a smart move. We're going to hire someone to repaint the whole place this summer. We thought about tearing off the old siding and replacing it, but then that runs into the regulations on whether it can be considered a historical home."

Joe's mom clucked. "It's like ours. It's not as big as your place, but it's added value to have that historical designation."

"Don't I know. Just sanding off, I don't know thirty coats of paint over the centuries, will take some time," I replied.

"Good for you. I'm glad you all are doing that. It's a lovely home," Maria offered.

Joey called over to Joe about his game, and Joe squeezed my knee. "I'll be back."

His father followed him into the living room, leaving me alone in the kitchen with his mother. I braced myself. She didn't waste any time.

"Do you talk to your father? You all have been through a lot these past few years, with your mother passing away and then what happened with your father. I'm very sorry about your mother."

I took a breath and a swallow of the water she'd given me as I nodded. "Definitely. I miss my mother. And…" Gah, I was nervous. I took another breath, trying to keep my nerves calm. "Look, I was young in high school, and I didn't really know what to do when my dad said I couldn't date Joe. I didn't want to hurt Joe, and I'm so sorry. I'm sure you think…" I paused and collected my thoughts. "Well, I don't know what you think. My dad was not a nice man then, and he's not a nice man now. I'm really sorry."

Joe's mom was in the middle of checking on the casserole in the oven. She closed the oven door quickly before turning to face me. Her eyes were warm, and I felt a little bit of relief slide through me. "It's okay. Joe was heartbroken, but you were just a girl. For what it's worth, there's something to be said for respecting your parents even if what he asked of you wasn't the right thing. You were young, and this is a small town. I don't have any idea how you could have tried to sneak around after that." She rolled her eyes. "I'm definitely glad you two found each other again, though. Joe is very happy. How did it go with Joey this weekend so far?"

"Okay, I think. He's a good boy."

She smiled. "Most of the time. I'm sure he's on his best behavior. He was very excited to meet you. He knows his dad loves you."

"How do you feel about it?" I asked.

She crossed the kitchen and rested her hand on my shoulder. "Joe loves you. This isn't too soon. It's been months now, and it's not like you two are new to each other. You're the first woman he's introduced to Joey, so I hope you understand how much that means."

Holy hell. No pressure or anything. I nodded. "I do."

She gave my shoulder another squeeze before stepping back, and I helped her prep the salad. I started to relax until she commented, "Joey has been wanting a little brother or sister. Maybe after you and Joe move on to getting married first. That'll be exciting for him."

She said this the way people who could have children spoke, calmly and as if it was an expectation.

Fuck. I hoped my expression didn't show my panic. My stomach tightened into a painful knot instantly, and I took a breath, managing to nod and make a noncommittal noise.

"Do you want children?" she pressed.

"Oh, yes," I said quickly because that was the truth. I just had no idea how she would feel if she knew I couldn't have children.

Chapter Nineteen

JOE

One month later

I stared at the ring, turning it over in my hand. Even though I had already told Thea I planned to ask her to marry me, I was really going to do it this weekend. I'd taken Joey with me to pick out the ring, and he was sworn to secrecy. However, I promised him I'd ask her soon. He was spending tonight with my parents, which he did on occasion anyway. My dad was going to take him out fishing early tomorrow, so it was easier if he was staying there.

Now came the hard part. We were going to have dinner at Bay Bistro. After that, I planned to take her for a walk on the beach. Way back when, in high school, we used to walk on the beach a lot. It was a great place to make out.

I returned to my en-suite bathroom and glanced in the mirror to check my appearance before chuckling to myself. I wasn't worried about Thea being attracted to me, but here I was anxious about asking her to marry me.

An hour later, Thea was seated across from me at a table in Bay Bistro. I felt her foot nudge my calf. "Look."

When I glanced out the windows, the sun was setting, casting a shimmer of orange and gold across the ocean's surface. "It's so pretty. Makes me want to go for a swim," she commented.

"Uh, do you remember how cold the water is here?" I asked.

"I do, but I also remember how awesome it feels to dive in the ocean on really hot days."

Memories flashed through my mind of summer afternoons on the beach with her. I reached over to catch her hand in mine. She bit her lip. "You look beautiful."

"Really?"

"That's not the kind of thing I lie about," I said, completely serious.

"I had a busy day at work. After the train ride, I was feeling kind of frumpy when I got here."

"I can't tell."

"You're good to me, Joe." Her lips curled in a warm smile.

"And you're good to me."

The server arrived to clear our plates, asking if we wanted dessert. Thea waggled her eyebrows. "Do we want the chocolate thing?"

"We can take it home."

"Perfect."

She smiled up at the server. "I forgot what it's called, but we want that ridiculous chocolate thing to go with extra syrup."

Our server grinned. "That would be the chocolate mousse with a brownie center. I'll be back with that and the check in a few minutes."

"What's our plan this weekend?" she asked after he departed. "I thought Joey was with you."

"He'll be here tomorrow. He's spending the night with my parents. He does that sometimes."

A major bonus to easing Thea into meeting my son was we didn't have to alternate weekends anymore. For the first time since I'd been a father, I was getting a sense of what it felt like to expand my little family bubble. It wasn't that I didn't feel like Joey and I were a family. We were, and that included my parents as well, but I hadn't been able to share parenting with anyone in my day-to-day life. Of late, his mother had also been busier than usual and even asked me to take him some during her weeks. I kept meaning to make time to talk to her, but my life was as busy as ever.

"So, I have you all to myself tonight?" Thea teased a few minutes later as we walked out of the restaurant.

"Absolutely. You also get me all to yourself when I come down there for the weekends."

"I've been thinking," she began once we were in my SUV.

"You're always thinking," I teased lightly.

She rolled her eyes. "Joe, I'm serious."

"Okay. What are you serious about?"

I had just started the vehicle, but I didn't put it in gear and turned to face her.

"What do you think about me moving up here?"

My heart thudded hard as though pumping a fist in joy, but I kept my expression neutral. This was a loaded topic, especially for Thea.

"I want you to know this is not an expectation for me," I said carefully.

"I know it's not," she said, her cheeks flushing slightly. "But while I like Boston and I like being near my friends, the more time I spend here, the more I just can't wait until I can come here. Even on the weekends when you come to Boston, I'd rather us be up here. It won't be easy, but I could just start my own small law practice here."

"Are you serious?"

She nodded quickly. "Absolutely. I've looked into my options. It'd be really hard to start my own law practice in Boston because so many large firms are already there. I don't love working for a big firm. I enjoy my work, but my job can feel like being in one of those revolving doors where I just spin around and around from one case to the next. Money would be tight, but I think I could do it here. What do you think about that?"

My heart was punching both fists in the air now, but I forced myself to stay measured. "I think that'd be great, but it's really important to me that you know I don't expect this."

"I know, Joe. That's why I can think

about it. My lease runs out next January. I could see where things are at by then around work. With that timing, we wouldn't be rushing anything with Joey."

I wanted Thea to move in yesterday, but I had to consider my son, so I wouldn't rush it. I leaned over, cupping her chin lightly before I pressed a lingering kiss on her lips.

"I love that idea," I murmured as I lifted my head. "I absolutely love it. We've got plenty of time, and that gives you time to plan."

We smiled at each other, and for a split second, I felt like the giddy teenager I'd been after our first kiss.

"All right, you promised me a walk on the beach tonight," she said.

THEA

Summers in Maine meant warm days and cool nights. A soft breeze gusted off Haven's Bay as we walked along the beach. The dark gray sand was scattered with rocks. We'd frequented this stretch of beach between Joe's new house and my old family home when we were together. We didn't have much spending money back then, so we'd often go for walks.

"Do you think our place is still there?" I asked just as the wind caught my hair and spun it in a swirl. I lifted my free hand, brushing it back.

"Of course, it's still there. The rocky ledges aren't likely to go anywhere soon."

I grinned. "Do you think anybody else has found it?"

Joe shrugged. "Maybe not, but I'd guess so. I'm not up for chasing off teenagers tonight, so I hope we have it to ourselves."

"Oh, are we planning to make out?" I teased.

A giddy sense of joy rose inside my chest, and a sense of lightness gusted like a soft breeze through me. Finally telling Joe that I'd been thinking about moving up here was such a relief and felt so freeing. It felt right. He was so careful to make sure I understood he didn't expect me to. He'd gone out of his way to make it seem like it would be no big deal if we got married and I commuted to Boston forever. That wasn't what I wanted, though. I wanted a life with Joe.

This was the right move for me, and it felt really good. Now that I'd voiced my plans aloud, I was almost annoyed that my lease didn't run out until after Christmas. That said, it probably was for the best. I didn't want to rush too much as far as Joey was concerned. While I could move up here and bang around my family's home by myself, it would be nice to move right in with Joe.

A few minutes later, the shoreline curved, and we approached the edge of a cliff. Joe's hand was warm around mine as we walked around a cluster of rocks with the sand damp under our shoes. The tide was out and wouldn't come in for hours. A moment later, a sheltered outcropping of rocks was revealed. It was still there, just as he assured me.

I squealed. "It's here!"

He smiled down at me, stopping and pressing a fierce kiss to my lips. "I thought it would be."

I leaned back to peer up at him. "We can kiss, but it has to be standing up. We're not sixteen anymore, and we don't need to deal with the sand."

Joe's laughter sent a blazing shiver through me. "Making out on the sand isn't what I'm after."

I glanced around, my eyes scanning until I found the spot. Along the outer edge where the ledge hung over the rocks, we'd scratched our initials.

Joe grinned. "Still there. It's probably more permanent than carving them on a tree."

"Definitely. I never thought I'd come back here," I said, glancing up at him.

"No?" he pressed, his tone low and soft.

I took a deep breath when my chest tightened with a sting of pain. "No, this was our place, and it hurt that we broke up."

Still holding his hand, I turned to look out at the ocean, breathing in the crisp salty air. Seagulls were calling in the distance, and a crow was somewhere nearby, chattering right back at them. The wind blew my hair back from my face, and I watched as a wave broke on the shoreline. The sun was a golden ball of fire in the sky, just about to disappear behind the horizon.

When I looked back at Joe, his eyes were waiting for mine, and he held something in his free hand.

"What is it?" I asked.

He began to move as if to bend down on one knee, and I squeezed his hand tightly. "Are you...?"

He kneeled before uncurling his hand. A beautiful white gold band with an emerald-cut diamond in a solitaire setting lay there. I slapped my palm to my chest, my lungs seizing as my heart sputtered to a stop and then lunged, my pulse speeding so hard and fast my entire body was reverberating.

"I love you. I already told you I was going to ask you to marry me. I thought this was the perfect place because it is *our* place. This is actually the first time I've walked back since the last time I was here with you," he explained.

I didn't realize I was crying until I felt a tear roll down my cheek. I brushed it away with my knuckles.

"Will you marry me?" Joe asked. "I want it all with you—the good, the boring, and the not so easy. I know we can do it."

I didn't even have to think. "Yes, yes," I whispered hoarsely.

He slid the ring on my shaky finger as I held it out before standing and looping his arms around my waist. I took a deep breath, pressing my lips at the base of his throat before looking up at him.

"I love you, and we already have a plan."

"A plan for what?" he prompted, a smile teasing at the corners of his mouth.

"I'm coming back home."

His smile was sunlight shining down into my heart. "I love you," he murmured before bending low to kiss me.

By the time he lifted his head, I was breathless. He'd copped a feel of my bottom and slid his other hand up under my shirt. I giggled. "We're not doing it here." I gestured to the sand below our feet.

"Let's go home."

We walked back along the beach as the sun disappeared behind the horizon, and the stars began to appear in the dusky sky as darkness came to claim it. We made good use of Joe's bed that night.

The next morning, I looked over at him enjoying waffles because that was definitely his breakfast specialty, and asked, "Did Joey know?"

"Know what?"

I rolled my eyes. "That you were going to ask me to marry you this weekend."

"He didn't know it was going to be last night because if I told him, I wouldn't have been able to persuade him to go with my parents. He knew it was coming because I took him with me to help pick out the ring."

"Are you serious?" I sputtered.

He shrugged. "Totally. It's very important to him. Honestly, if you're really into the big wedding planning thing, he's going to be heartbroken if you don't include him."

I threw my head back with a laugh as joy rose inside. "I'm kind of probably in the middle on that. I really don't want to go crazy like some people do, but I would like to have something. I feel like we waited a long time to get here. Joey can help me plan it all."

Chapter Twenty-One

THEA

Joey looked at me solemnly. His feet didn't even touch the floor where he sat on a bench at the wedding planner's office. He was very excited. The woman helping us had stepped out to get some samples for color schemes and flowers.

Meanwhile, Joey looked over at me. "When do I get a brother or a sister?"

I had just taken a swallow of water, and I choked on it, sputtering inelegantly and getting water all over my knees and the bottom of my shirt. I cleared my throat and grabbed a napkin on the table, quickly dabbing at my shirt and knees and scanning around to discover I hadn't gotten water on anything but myself.

"Excuse me?" I finally said when I looked back at Joey.

"Now that you and Dad are getting married, you can have a baby next, right?"

Fuck, fuck, fuck, fuck, fuck. My stomach turned sickly, and I took a deep breath as a shaft of pain sliced through my heart. "Um, I don't know. Things don't always happen in order like that."

Joe and I had talked several times about this, and he kept assuring me that he was completely on board with adoption, but how did I explain this to Joey? I sure as hell didn't want to do it here in the wedding planner's office.

Joey stared over at me expectantly. "When your dad and I figure out what's going to happen next, it may or may not involve a brother or sister. No matter what, you'll be the first to know."

Joey was no dummy, and he eyed me skeptically. I was beyond relieved when the wedding planner returned to the room at that moment. She effectively distracted him by asking for his assistance in planning the children's menu.

Later that night at Joe's house, Joey was sound asleep, and we were in bed.

Joe's palm swept down my back, and he

cupped my bottom, giving it a dirty squeeze. "Come on, sweetheart, ride me," he murmured.

I needed no further instruction and shimmied closer, rising up as he positioned himself at my entrance. I let out a satisfied moan as I sank down over his thick length, wiggling my hips for good measure once he was seated fully inside me.

His head thumped against the wall. "Fuck, Thea. You feel so good," he rasped.

God, I didn't think I'd ever get tired of how good it was with us. It was just easy, and the sex was this incredible combination of sexy, dirty, sometimes filthy, but also sensual and sweet. It was everything I needed. Joe made me feel like the most womanly woman I'd ever felt. It was only minutes later that I was crying out as my release wracked me. I rippled around his cock, savoring the sound of his own ragged cry and the feel of his release filling me.

I fell against him, tucking my head into his neck and lazily dropping a kiss right there as I caught my breath.

"Do we really have to wait until January?" he asked a few minutes later.

I lifted my head, smiling. "Well, that's when my notice ends. I timed it with my lease. I might be willing to skip out on my lease, but I don't feel right about leaving my job in a lurch. I have to finish up that one case."

"God, I hate that you're so responsible," he teased.

"As if you aren't," I countered with a grin.

Just then, as if to prove my point, his emergency phone buzzed on the table beside the bed. He was covering the emergency call service for the weekend.

"You're right. In fact, I'm so responsible that right now, I'm going to take that call, and I might have to leave."

"I know. I hate that you're so responsible, but I also love it," I said with a smile.

I shimmied off his lap, walking into the bathroom to clean up. He was on my heels seconds later, taking what he called a thirty-second shower. The man was out the door within five minutes after his phone rang. I plunked down on his couch and turned on the television. That was usually my habit when he got a call, unless I somehow slept through it, which was rare. As I waited for him to return, my mind kept replaying that conversation with Joey at the wedding planner's office.

I needed to tell Joe about it, and I knew I

needed to find a way to explain to Joey that I could not have children. And, hell, I was anxious even talking to Joe about it because that tiny doubt in the back of my mind still wondered if he was just appeasing me on this issue.

———

A week later, the paper crinkled under my legs as I sat up on the examining table at my gynecologist's office. She was peeling the latex gloves off her hands and putting them in the trash receptacle. She looked over at me.

I took a breath and rolled my shoulders back.

"I'm just your doctor, but I'm going to tell you this because it is so much the truth. Love is love is love is love. Some people have biological children who never should, there are people who adopt and create amazing families for their children, and some people never have children and are very happy with that. IVF isn't an option for you. I mentioned it before, but I'm going to remind you again. You can call that therapist we talked about."

I didn't cry. I was pretty much out of tears. As if to pour cold water on the dream of the life I wanted with Joe, his mother had asked me about kids again. And even worse, little Joey had come in during the conversation. I hadn't even known how to say any of the things I needed to say.

Adding another layer of anxiety, Joe had told me last weekend that Joey's mom had asked him about having a talk. He hadn't wanted to do it when I wasn't there. I appreciated that, but not knowing what it was about was stressing me right the hell out.

I'd waited in his office at the garage while he met with her. I had no idea what they talked about because all he'd told me was she had some health concerns. She was Joey's mother, and I was panicking.

I kicked my thoughts off that self-defeating track and hurried out of the doctor's office. I didn't need to get all worked up over Joey's mother. Joe didn't even call her his ex. I knew he sensed my insecurities around it because he had reminded me more than once that I had nothing to worry about.

I just felt so ridiculous about the whole thing. Just as I hit the sidewalk, my phone vibrated in my purse. I slipped it out, glancing down to see Joe calling. My lips started to curl into a smile automatically. Even though he was hours away in Haven's

Bay, he was very attentive. He called me every day, insisting texts weren't enough. I loved it.

Aside from the attention, it reminded me of the way we'd been before. When we were in high school, he'd called me every chance he could. That was way back before cell phones, and I was limited to fifteen-minute phone calls. That was one thing my father hadn't interfered with before he blew our relationship up because he was hardly ever home, so he didn't know Joe called me every night.

I slipped my thumb across the screen and lifted the phone to my ear. "Hello."

"Hey, sweetheart. Are you taking the train up tomorrow?"

"That's the plan."

"Perfect. Why don't I pick you up there?"

"You don't have to make the drive, Joe."

"I know I don't, but it's summer, and the weather's gorgeous. I thought we could stop at our favorite lobster roll truck on the way back. We can sit at the picnic tables and listen to the seagulls."

I giggled.

"Seagulls are romantic, you know," he teased.

"Of course."

"So, what do you say?"

"You don't actually think I'd say no to that, do you?"

"Sweetheart, I don't take anything for granted with you." His voice was low, and it felt as if he reached into my chest and squeezed my heart.

Emotion rushed through me, tightening in my throat. As solid as my feelings for Joe were, this was a lot. I felt as if I were walking an emotional tightrope, trying not to get too joyful.

"I'd love that," I finally said.

Someone jostled me as they hurried by on the sidewalk.

"How was your day?" he asked.

"Busy with work. That's all."

I wasn't about to fill him in on my conversation with my doctor. He didn't need to know I was still holding on to futile hopes.

"What about your day?" I pressed, injecting lightness into my tone.

"It was a paperwork day, and I had to run over to our offices in Brunswick and Bangor."

"If you're busy, that's a good thing."

"It is. Speaking of that, we've got some extra office space in my dad's original garage downtown."

"What do you mean the original garage?

Is that the one near downtown where you have your office?"

"Nope, that's the newer old garage. You were probably too little to remember, but my dad used to have a small garage on Main Street. There was literally just enough room for one car to pull in. It's in that old brick building just past the green. Way back then, my parents lived upstairs in the small apartment."

"Oh, wow. No, I don't remember that. Your family still owns the building?"

"We sure do. It's part of the business. Over the years, we've done a couple of different things with it. It's no longer a garage. The upstairs is converted into an apartment rental, and the downstairs is office space. Right now, two accountants share it, but one of them is moving out of town. I just wanted to put it out there so that you might think about it for your office."

"Joe, I can't move until January." It was sweet for him to try to help me plan for my eventual law practice there, but we had months to go. "It would feel weird for me if you held the space that long."

"We don't charge anybody rent there."

"What?!" I exclaimed.

"Seriously, it was paid off forever ago. The

accountant is my dad's old friend. The one who's moving out of town is his son. He's getting married, and his wife-to-be lives in Portland. The guy staying would prefer we don't look into renting it out to just anyone. He'd rather it be somebody he knows."

"Does he hate my father?" I asked. I glanced up, checking the crosswalk light at the intersection. It was green, so I kept on walking.

"I will ask him if he hates your father. Is that a deal breaker for you? Because I don't think he would blame it on you," Joe said.

"I just don't want it to be weird."

A horn honked. Distracted, I glanced over to see someone had fallen off a bicycle. "Joe, I need to go. Somebody fell off their bicycle, and I want to help them up."

"What time does your train get in tomorrow?"

"Five thirty."

"I'll be there. Love you."

"Love you," I returned.

Slipping my phone into my purse, I hurried over and helped the woman up from her bicycle.

"It was nobody's fault but mine," she said as I fetched her backpack from the pavement and handed it over.

"Are you okay?" I asked.

She was already on her feet and checking out her bike. She held out one leg and pointed down to the abraded spot on her skin. "Could have been much worse."

"Definitely not too bad. Some clean up and a little ibuprofen should help," I offered.

I waited until she was on her bike and pedaling away. The sunlight glinted on my engagement ring as I lifted my hand to brush my hair back.

Chapter Twenty-Two

THEA

"Oh, my god. That was so good," I moaned as I wiped my mouth with a napkin.

I had just finished a buttery lobster roll. A salty breeze gusted off the ocean as Joe nodded in agreement. He paused to take a swallow of water and glanced down at the little plastic basket sitting in front of me.

"How come you only got one?" he asked.

"Because one is enough."

Joe had gotten two lobster rolls. He lifted the second one, shrugging and commenting, "Your loss."

"Would you share with me?"

He'd just opened his mouth to take a bite and lowered the roll as he closed his mouth. "I don't know. I love you, but these are good lobster rolls, and you can always get your own."

I kicked his foot under the table. "I don't want another one, but if that's a test of love, you failed."

He rolled his eyes and took another bite. A seagull called nearby, and I glanced out over the ocean. It wasn't that late, and the sun was just starting to lower in the sky. We were about halfway between where Joe picked me up in Wells and Haven's Bay. Maine's coastline was scattered with seafood restaurants and food trucks, such as this one.

This one was in a small parking lot near an old car garage. They specialized in lobster rolls and didn't serve anything else. Lobster rolls were divine, especially dripping in butter. It felt good to have a carefree evening. I realized that next summer, Joe and I could explore on our own, branching out from our weekends. It would be nice to go home to him every night.

A few minutes later, we were driving again, and Joe's phone rang. The dashboard lit up with the name of Joey's mom. His eyes angled to mine. "I don't want to get this, but I should. Do you mind?"

"No, go for it." I didn't mind, in part because him having the conversation in front of me meant he wasn't hiding anything. He lifted his phone, answering, "Hey, Vanessa. What's up?"

He nodded along to something she said. "I'll take care of it. I already told you I would. When is he coming to stay with me?" he asked after another pause.

"All right, that'll work. Thanks for keeping me in the loop."

He ended the call, and my curiosity was burning up inside. "Is everything okay?"

Joe shrugged. "Yes and no. Vanessa's going through some stuff. Joey's gonna come stay with me for three months."

"Oh, that's great. Right?"

"I think so. I love having him. I'll have to do a little scrambling to make sure daycare's covered, but my mom will help out."

"Oh." I couldn't mask the surprise in that single word.

Joe glanced over quickly, his smile reassuring. "I'm surprised too. I planned to talk to you about it this weekend, so I guess we're talking now. It'll be good for him to be there, I think. Do you mind?"

"Of course not!" I exclaimed, meaning it completely.

I was just puzzled as to how this came about, even more so that I hadn't heard a thing about it until this very moment. "Is everything okay with his mom?"

He shrugged. "She's just got some stuff going on."

Joe had to look forward by necessity because he was approaching the stoplight. I tried not to interpret the hint of evasiveness in his tone and told myself it was nothing.

"Have you ever had Joey for that long before?" I heard myself asking.

I didn't like the uncertainty I was feeling.

"Not for this long."

This conversation was effectively derailed when Joe slowed to turn into Haven's Bay Grocery. "I haven't had a chance to go to the grocery store." He glanced my way. "Want to come in with me?"

"Of course."

He grinned, and we walked in together. I smiled as I glanced around. This wasn't the first time I'd been here recently, but it still brought back a sense of nostalgia. The original store had been expanded substantially.

"They even have a new deli counter," I commented, smiling up at Joe.

He squeezed my hand and winked. The original store was basically a corner of the space now. In that section, they'd kept the old hardwood floors and the pressed tin ceiling, including the small pharmacy lunch counter with an old-school lemonade maker. The rest of it was modernized and quadruple the size. Even though Haven's Bay was still a small town, it wasn't as small as it used to be.

We got a cart, and it was actually fun to go through the store with Joe. It was something we hadn't done during our weekends together. It felt mundane and somehow intimate.

"I don't even know. Do you have a milk preference?" he asked when we stopped in front of the selection.

I shook my head. "I usually go with the store brand. It's the cheapest option."

"Same."

He grabbed two gallons, and I glanced up, my eyes widening. "I need it to get me through next week. And you know I like cereal for breakfast during the week."

I burst out laughing. "That's a lot of milk."

We kept on shopping. "Should we get takeout here for dinner?" he asked as he slowed in front of the expanded deli section. "They have really good pizza."

"Let's."

With Joe wheeling the cart, we made our way to the counter. I grinned when I saw

Sherry Levesque behind the register. "You're everywhere," I teased after she finished ringing up a pair of teenage girls in front of us.

She smiled. "You know me, I like to keep my eyes on every place."

"Do you own more than this, Emile's, and Bay Bistro?"

She shook her head. "Absolutely not. My daughter wants to expand and open another place, but I told her that it's going to be all on her."

"You all have really made this grocery store a nice place. I love that you kept the original space the way it's always been," I commented.

"We knew we needed to expand. We figured if we kept this part as a small café, it was a way to honor how it started. You know Emile's grandparents started it."

"I know," I replied.

"It's over seventy-five years old," Sherry added.

"And still going strong," Joe chimed in with a grin.

"Now, what can I get you two? Any minute now, there's going to be a line."

"Pizza, please," I said.

"We have full ones premade, or you can

get slices, whatever your preference is. If you want something made, it's probably going to be about a twenty-minute wait," she explained.

"What do you have premade?" Joe asked.

Sherry smiled. "Pepperoni, and I know that's your favorite."

"Let's get two larges then unless you want something else." He looked at me quickly.

"You know I love pepperoni."

While Sherry boxed the pizzas, she commented to Joe, "So I hear you're gonna have little Joey for a few months." When he nodded, she continued, "I hope everything's gonna be okay with his mom."

Sherry cast a quick glance at me, and I felt as if she were assessing me. I didn't even know what I didn't know, but I knew I didn't know *something* now.

Joe simply replied, "Oh, I'm sure it'll be fine."

His tone was almost too casual, and that sense of uncertainty curdled in my stomach uncomfortably. None of it made sense. Emotionally and intellectually, I knew it was ridiculous for me to wonder what was going on with Joey's mom. It was none of my business. But what didn't I know?

I lay in bed that night, awake and listening to the sound of Joe's even breathing. We'd had a good night together, enjoying pizza and watching a movie. Since Joey was not here tonight, Joe had teased me to a shattering orgasm on the couch before carrying me into the bedroom and making me fly yet again. It was easy to forget myself, to lose my worries in our fiery connection.

Except now I couldn't sleep. I felt left out of whatever was going on. And oddly, even though I'd told Joe more than once that my lease wasn't up until January and I couldn't move until then because of my job, part of me wished he'd thought to ask me to come earlier. I could help take care of Joey.

"Well, maybe not," I grumbled to myself.

I rolled over, looking out the window. Joe had this house designed with an excellent view of the ocean from the bedroom. Stars blinked at me in the darkness, and a crescent-shaped moon hung in the sky, the pearly sliver of light rippling on the dark waters beneath. I resolved to ask Joe more directly what was going on.

Chapter Twenty-Three

JOE

"I'm curious, this just kind of seems out of the blue with Joey coming to stay with you for a few months. Is everything really okay with his mom?" Thea asked, her tone carefully casual.

Ah, hell. No, everything was not okay with my son's mother, but I had promised her I would keep it private. I knew Vanessa didn't even want to tell me what the hell was going on, but I'd demanded it when she'd asked me if he could stay for a few months. After hemming and hawing and trying to hold me off, she finally told me.

Vanessa was going to rehab. First, she was spending a full month in an inpatient setting. Then they would assess if she was ready to transition into something like a halfway house. She'd actually gotten arrested for an OUI and possession. The police had pulled her over when she was high as a kite on opiates. Her lawyer had worked out some kind of deal for her to do treatment in lieu of more time. Maine had pretty strict OUI laws. Apparently, this was her second offense, which was news to me.

I was furious that she hadn't told me about the first one. I was doing my damnedest to understand that she was trying to do the right thing. I didn't like keeping this a secret from Thea or from my parents.

I held Thea's gaze and nodded. "Look, I don't have all the details." Okay, that was true because I really didn't. All I had was a sketch of what was going on. "She just needs to take care of some things. I'd love to have Joey full-time as it is, so I'm glad I can have him now."

Thea's eyes searched mine. I sensed she knew I wasn't telling her the whole truth, and I only hoped she would respect why when I could finally explain.

"Is something going on with his mom that you haven't mentioned?" she asked next.

Fuck. "Thea, no." I tried to tell myself I wasn't lying. But I *was*, and my conscience stung.

She blinked and looked down, idly dragging her fork through the syrup on her plate as she nodded. "Okay, well if you need any help, let me know."

"Of course."

That uncomfortable conversation ended, and we went on about our day. The rest of the weekend felt good. If Thea was dwelling on the news about Joey coming to stay with me full-time, she didn't let on. The only other time we discussed it was in planning whether I should bring him to Boston. She insisted that didn't make sense and that it was easier for her to come up to Haven's Bay.

Another weekend later, I convinced myself we were fine. I took Joey with me to pick Thea up at the train station in Wells. On the way back to Haven's Bay, we stopped and had lobster rolls. I looked over at her just as the wind caught her hair and spun it in a swirl. She was laughing, and she was beautiful, and everything felt just right. The girl who'd become the woman I loved was here, my son was here, and we felt like a family. I could imagine how it was going to be when she moved up here for good.

The weekend was great until I had to leave Saturday night to deal with an emergency call. Thea was going to make sure Joey got to bed. She knew the routine, and it wasn't like there was much to it at his age. I left on the emergency call without any worry.

I came home two hours later to hear him yelling, "You're not my mom! You can't tell me what to do."

I walked down the hallway to discover Thea standing in Joey's bedroom doorway. Her eyes met mine briefly, her expression controlled. Joey's face was blotchy.

"What's going on?" I asked, focusing on my son.

"She's trying to make me go to bed," he whined.

"Yeah, your bedtime was an hour ago, and you should already be asleep."

"She can't tell me what to do. She's not my mom," he muttered, his expression sullen.

"Joey, Thea is not trying to be your mom. Just like when you have a babysitter or when you're at Grammy's, you need to go to bed when it's bedtime. I told you Thea was in charge."

He burst into tears again, and she quickly backed out of the door. I caught her hand and gave it a reassuring squeeze before she walked down the hallway.

"Joey," I began.

He was sitting on his bed and turned his

back to me, curling into a ball. This wasn't the first time he'd had a more emotional moment than I expected. I knew he didn't really understand what was going on with his mom. I also didn't know precisely how she explained it to him. I crossed the room to sit on his bed.

"Joey." His narrow shoulders were shaking when I placed my palm on his back, and my heart twisted sharply.

He finally stopped crying a few minutes later. The tears slowed, the shaking stopped, and he lifted his head. "Will you tell Thea I'm sorry?"

"You can tell her in the morning. You still need to go to bed."

"I want my mom." He sniffled.

"I know you do. You have your phone call with her tomorrow afternoon, but it'll have to wait until then."

"I don't want to talk to Mom when Thea is here," he mumbled, putting his forehead on his knees.

"She'll be leaving in the morning. Even if she's here, it's okay if you talk to your mom."

"No, because her being here is like her trying to be my mom."

"Joey, your mom is your mom no matter

who you're staying with or who I'm seeing," I said clearly and slowly.

"Why can't Mom come stay with you if she's having a hard time?"

"Because that's not an option. Your mom and I are not together that way. You know that."

My heart twisted at the disappointment on his face. After another moment, he angled toward me, and I slipped my arm around his shoulders. He fell asleep right there within a few minutes. I carefully shifted him, getting him situated under the covers. He never woke.

When I walked out to the living room, Thea wasn't there, so I ventured back to the master bedroom. She was in the bathroom washing her face. When she lifted her head, her eyes locked with mine in the mirror. Dabbing at her face with a towel, she said, "I'm fine."

"He said to tell you he's sorry, but I suggested he apologize in the morning."

She nodded as she straightened. After she dried her hands, she carefully put the towel on the rack, seeming to move with deliberation.

When she turned to face me, I rested my hands on the counter, caging her in my arms.

As I dipped my head to press my forehead against hers, I murmured, "Sorry, he's struggling a little right now."

"Joe, what's going on with Vanessa?"

When I lifted my head, her gaze was serious. "I can't tell you everything," I finally said. "Not because I don't want to, but because she asked me to keep it private. It's not mine to tell."

Her eyes softened, and she lifted a hand, smoothing her fingers over the crease between my brows. "Okay," she whispered. "I understand."

Relief rippled through me. I kissed her, diving into the fire that I knew was so easy to kindle between us. I needed to forget my worries. That wasn't difficult. Our chemistry burned so hot that touching was like tossing a match in a puddle of gasoline with us.

Chapter Twenty-Four

THEA

I never said anything else to Joe about what happened. It wasn't a big deal. Children all over the world got fussy about bedtime. Plenty of children had moms and dads, and moms and moms, and dads and dads, and any combination of family members going through things.

My emotional reaction wasn't rational, and I knew that. I hated that I was feeling so out of sorts. Every time I tried to logic my way out of the trains of thought boxing me in, I failed. Because I couldn't have children. Even if I could be the most amazing step-mother in the world to Joey, it wouldn't change what I could never be to any child.

I still didn't know what was going on with

his mom, and that lack of knowledge felt like a splinter driven under the edge of a fingernail. It was causing just enough pain to hurt, but a minor enough injury that I kept ignoring it.

Joey did apologize the following morning. He didn't even need to, but of course I accepted it. It was no big deal. It really wasn't. My own freaking feelings were the problem, and those had nothing to do with Joey.

When something came up for Joe the following weekend because he had to cover the car service the whole weekend, I told him maybe it was best if I didn't come up. I changed my mind and went up anyway because, of course, he needed someone to be there for Joey. I didn't want to be that kind of fiancée, the kind who stayed out of the way when it was difficult.

Joey got upset and reminded me I wasn't his mother again. "I know that, Joey. I'm not trying to be your mom."

I was folding his laundry, and Joe was out on a call, dealing with towing three cars that had what sounded like a spectacular fender bender near the town green.

"Why are you here every weekend?" Joey crossed his arms, his cheeks puffing up as he stared at me.

"Your dad and I are engaged, and I love him."

"I changed my mind. I don't want you and Dad to get married."

I felt lost in this conversation, but I couldn't avoid it, so I handled it as best I could.

"Sweetie." I placed one of his T-shirts on the top of the stack and knelt in front of him. "Nothing is going to happen too fast. I'll let your dad know how you're feeling. Will that help.?"

A little tuft of hair bounced on top of his head with his emphatic nod. "And can you leave?"

"I can't leave now, Joey."

"You can call Grammy. She'll come over."

I felt a little sick, and my heart ached. This, I could logically understand. Maybe I didn't understand what was going on with his mom, but I knew Joey somehow thought if he pinned his hopes on his mom and his dad being together, then whatever was happening with his mom would be solved. Maybe a little information would have helped me, but still.

"I'll wait and talk to your dad," I said calmly.

"I think you should go when he gets home."

I kept my promise and talked to Joe when he got home after Joey was asleep in bed. I even suggested it'd be best if I left.

"Are you insane? You're not leaving," Joe said firmly.

"Joe, he's really upset."

I swallowed and tried to ignore the twisty feeling in my stomach.

"I know, but—" Joe shifted on the couch and ran a hand through his hair. "I know he's upset, but he can't dictate what the grown-ups in his life are going to do."

"I know. It seems like he's feeling really emotional," I finally said.

"I know he is, but this isn't okay. I'm going to talk to him tomorrow."

"I think you should wait to talk to him until after I leave."

"Why would I wait until after you leave?"

"He's just a little boy. It's not logical, but he's connecting my presence here right now somehow to what's happening with his mom. I think it's best if you give him that space just for you and him to have the conversation."

Joe straightened, his brow creasing. "Thea, I think it's better if he hears it when we're here together. He needs to apologize to you for his feelings."

"Feelings are feelings. They're not rooted

in facts sometimes. He does *not* need to apologize to me for his feelings. That's confusing, and even adults can't fix their feelings like that. He's just a little boy."

Joe fell quiet after that. For the first time, it felt like we weren't on the same page. While part of me was comforted that he wanted us to be a united front with Joey, Joey needed to be able to process this with his dad. Not with me. That could come later.

Chapter Twenty-Five

JOE

"I don't care," Joey said, blinking rapidly as he stared at me. His tone was mulish, and his cheeks were blotchy, which meant he was about to cry.

"Joey, it's important that you respect Thea. She cares about you."

"She's not my mom. She's never going to be my mom!" he burst out.

"She knows that, and so do I. Tell me what's going on here. When I told you I wanted to marry her, you were excited. Now, you don't want her to visit, and you don't want me to marry her. I love her. She *is* going to be a part of our lives."

Joey burst into tears and spun away. As he

dashed down the hall, his feet thumped loudly on the hardwood flooring. He had a lightweight door, so it didn't slam very effectively, but he sure tried.

I stood, smoothing my hands over my jeans. Thea was right. This was a conversation I had needed to have with him privately. It still went straight to hell. I contemplated following him to his room but decided to give him a little space.

———

"What do you mean you're not coming?"

"With Joey with you full-time right now and his mom gone, I think it's all adding up to a bit much for him with me being there every weekend. He needs some time with you," Thea explained as I adjusted the phone between my ear and shoulder.

"He gets time with me. He's with me all the time right now, except when I'm at work."

"I know, I just… Joe, I don't know how to explain it, but I, I think we should take a few weeks off."

"What do you mean a few weeks off? Like a vacation," I practically growled.

Her sigh filtered through the phone line.

"The past few weekends I've been there, you know he gets emotional. It turns into a thing every time, and I feel like my presence is exacerbating the situation."

"Yeah, and he's a kid. That's gonna happen. He needs to be able to deal with you in my life. I can't put us on pause. It's gonna be okay. I just think—"

She cut in. "I don't even really know what's going on with his mom. I respect that she asked you to keep it private, but maybe he doesn't know either. Maybe that's part of the problem."

"I love you."

"I love you too. Let's take a few weekends off and regroup."

"Thea, I don't like this," I insisted. Tension coiled in a band around my chest, and I didn't like the uneasiness sliding through me.

"Look, this is hard for me too. It's confusing for me that you don't understand where I'm coming from. I'm thinking about Joey. He needs to come first."

"He always comes first," I practically snapped. "Maybe it's best if we stick with our routine."

"Joe, please. I love you. I'll talk to you tomorrow night, but I'm not coming up there."

"Thea—" I began.

"I love you," she repeated right before I heard the click that ended our call.

Chapter Twenty-Six

THEA

As soon as I ended the call, I took a few deep breaths. I couldn't even keep myself calm and burst into tears. I set the phone on the counter and curled my hands on the edge as I leaned over.

No matter what, I knew I was doing the right thing. Joe didn't have to tell me what was going on with Joey's mom, but he did need to give Joey a little time to adjust.

My phone vibrated on the counter, and I straightened, looking down to see Audrey's name flashing on the screen. I didn't even want to tell my friends about this. I swiped at my tears and ignored the call.

Joe called again, and I let it go to voice-mail. I resolved I was going to keep this boundary in place. Not for me, but for Joe and Joey.

A day later

"Sweetheart, come on. I talked to Joey. He's fine," Joe insisted.

"Tell me something, Joe. Does Joey know what's going on with his mom? No offense, but telling a kid his mom is having health issues or needs a break is vague as hell and will probably just create anxiety."

Joe's sigh was heavy, and I could picture him running his hand through his hair with his eyes weary and worried. My heart gave an achy thump. I loved him so much.

"Thea, I don't know exactly what his mom told him."

"Look, you don't have to tell me the details. I understand that she asked you to keep it private, but he needs to understand enough about what's happening. It might help him right now."

Now, I could imagine Joe was chewing the inside of his cheek with his lips twisting to the side. If I was right there in front of him, he would be glaring at me affectionately.

"Okay, okay, you might have a point," he finally said.

I loved being right. Hell, who didn't? But this wasn't even satisfying. I had too many emotions jumbled up. "I know I have a point. Maybe you could talk to her family or her and figure out how you guys will approach that. In the meantime, I'm going to keep staying down here for the weekends."

Chapter Twenty-Seven

JOE

I must have mulled over my conversation with Thea a few hundred times in a single day. Joey had reverted to form at home and hadn't had any emotional outbursts. Although I didn't like it, I grudgingly admitted to myself she had a point.

This situation was unsettling for Joey. I really didn't know what his mom had told him, and I was torn with how to approach her about it. Since we'd mostly cobbled together our co-parenting arrangement, we'd never been close in this way. We'd also been lucky enough not to have too many difficult issues arise.

I shifted my shoulders against the couch cushions. It was late, Joey was asleep, and I was idly watching television. At the moment, the car restoration show wasn't keeping me very occupied. I wasn't embarrassed that Joey's mom and I had never had a relationship, but I felt a little sheepish that a one-night stand resulted in him. Carelessness was what made me a father. It didn't change that I hadn't hesitated even for a millisecond to be a father to him.

This was the first time it felt like the carelessness of that one night was biting me in the ass. Because if I had more of a relationship with his mom, not romantic, but just anything other than logistical planning and checking in about our son, I would have thought to ask her exactly how she explained this situation to him.

Snagging my phone off the coffee table, I typed out a quick text to her.

Me: *I need to know what you told Joey. I know you told him you were going somewhere for help, but he's had a few struggles with it. I'd like to be more honest with him about what's going on. I respect that you want to be private, but we need to hash this out.*

I hit send before I could let myself think too much about it. I didn't expect to hear from her tonight. She generally wasn't too speedy to respond unless it was urgent.

I was surprised when my cell phone vibrated only five minutes or so later. Lifting it, I read her reply.

Vanessa: *I told him I needed some help. I didn't get into the details, but he knows I got pulled over because he was in the car.*

I silently swore. I'd learned that detail after the fact, and it still sent a jolt of cold anger through me, a blade of ice slicing through me. I'd talked to my therapist here, and she'd pointed out that kids generally know more than they let on. She'd given me some pointers on how to discuss issues such as substance abuse.

Me: *He needs to know more.*

Vanessa: *My only request is that we not get into the details about what I've been using.*

"Well, I don't even know that," I muttered to the phone.

I did know from her OUI records that she had failed a breathalyzer test and later tested positive for opiates in her system, but that was it.

Me: *Fine. I won't mention that. Do I have the all clear to talk with Joey?*

My thumbs hovered over the screen after I hit send. I wanted to ask her if she had said anything to him about us being together. In the past, she had a few times, and I'd asked her not to do that. I honestly didn't believe she wanted to be with me, but I knew she struggled with telling Joey things he didn't want to hear.

"Fuck it," I muttered to myself before tapping out another text.

Me: *Real quick, I know we've discussed it before, but has Joey asked you about us being together again? He's gotten a little emotional in ways that are surprising.*

Her reply came swiftly.

Vanessa: *First, yes you can talk to him. To your question... Sigh. Yes, I think you being engaged has brought up some feelings for him. I need to apologize. He once asked me what would happen if things didn't work out with you and Thea and if we'd ever be together. I told him I never knew what might happen with us. That's not a boundary I intended to cross. I need to practice being better about saying things he doesn't like to hear.*

I was a little surprised at her maturity. I stared at the text and decided to keep my reply brief.

Me: *Thank you for being honest. I'd appreciate it in the future if you didn't leave any doors open in his imagination on that. I'll let you know how it goes when I talk with him. Take care of yourself.*

Vanessa: *I hope this helps Joey understand.*

Joey crossed his arms, his lips pressing in a line while his cheeks puffed a little—a dead giveaway that he was upset and did not like what I'd said.

Fortunately, I knew he wouldn't, so I was completely prepared. A six-year-old's rage could be powerful although it was usually brief.

"Why?" he demanded.

"Because it's not going to happen," I replied, keeping my tone level and calm.

"But Mom—" he began, stopping when I shook my head.

"I talked to your mom."

"You did?" he cut in before I could get anything else out.

"By text, not in a phone conversation," I clarified.

He held his small hand out. "I want to see the text."

I shook my head. "No, it's private. Sometimes, your mom has a hard time saying things she thinks you might not like to hear. That's because she loves you." I hoped I'd kept a balance between being direct without bashing his mom there.

"What if you change your mind later? You

and Thea were together when you were in school, and then you weren't, and then you changed your mind."

Ah, I loved having a bright son, but sometimes, he was too logical. "That's a really good point, Joey." The tension in his face started to ease. Until I continued with, "But it doesn't change what's happening now. I love Thea, and I've loved her for years. I have no intention of not staying committed to her, and that's what matters right now in this situation. I know you miss your mom. Thea is not trying to be your mother, so you need to understand that."

He blinked really hard, pressing his lips together as if he had just eaten something horribly sour before turning his back to me.

I waited, and as I watched him, I saw his small shoulder blades begin to shake. Fuck. Now, my little boy was crying. He wasn't much of a crier. It pretty much cracked my heart into a million pieces whenever he did actually cry.

I stood from the couch and crossed over to him, squatting on my heels and placing my hand between his shoulder blades. They felt like tiny wings as they vibrated with his tremors. "It's okay," I said soothingly.

"But, bu-ut—" A noisy hiccup interrupted

him. "When is Mom coming home?" he finally asked between sniffles.

"What did she tell you?" I prompted him.

"She said three months."

"That's right. We can go look at the calendar."

"But she said that might change if something happened," he said, his voice still sniffly.

"It's possible, but you'll know way ahead if that happens, and it won't be a surprise. I know you miss your mom, Joey." I slid my hand up and down his back.

"She did something wrong, didn't she?"

"Yes and no. She has trouble sometimes, like the night when she was driving and you guys got pulled over by the police. Remember that?"

That little tuft of hair that tended to stick up wobbled with his nod. "She told me not to tell you, and I didn't like that. It made my stomach feel bad." He took a shuddering breath.

"Yeah, well, she needs a little help. Sometimes she does things to relax that aren't good for her."

Joey rolled his bottom lip, sucking it all the way into his mouth as he peered up at me. The tears had stopped, and I could see his little brain trying to absorb this information and make sense of it. How the hell did you explain addiction to a kid? Fuck, this was not easy.

"Okay. This didn't happen because of you and Thea?"

As soon as he asked that question, a bright light flicked on in my brain, awareness flashing in neon. "Uh, no, not at all. Thea and I didn't have anything to do with what's going on with your mom. I promise. Your mom will tell you the same thing."

I made a mental note to ask her to cover that in their phone call tonight. "Is that why you've been upset about Thea?"

He didn't break from my gaze, his eyes still searching mine, as if he was trying to figure out something, before he finally nodded. "Next time you're wondering about something like that, just ask me."

"Well, I used to ask Mom questions like why couldn't I tell you about the police thing, and she just said because it was a grown-up thing. I didn't know I could ask you."

"You can ask me anything. Some things are grown-up things, but I'll explain as best as I can and give you as much information as I can."

My son took another deep breath, letting

it out in a heaving sigh. "Is Thea coming back soon?"

"I hope so."

Joey's eyes dipped down, and he studied his shoes. "I like her."

"I know you do. Sometimes we can't get what we want. But Thea had nothing to do with your mom going away, I promise. Whether or not Thea's here, your mom and I are not going to be together like that."

My son lifted his eyes to mine, nodding solemnly. "Okay, well then I think you should call Thea and ask her to come up today."

That startled me enough that I let out a laugh. "Tonight? It's already Saturday, and she'll have to leave tomorrow."

"We can go to the train and get a lobster roll," he said hopefully.

I ruffled his hair. "We don't have time. You need to have your call with your mom tonight."

"Can she come next weekend? We could go to the pizza place, and I'll play in the play area, so you can be her date."

Now that he'd clarified his worries for the moment, he was back to himself.

"I will ask her about next weekend."

"Will you tell her about the date?"

Chapter Twenty-Eight

EPILOGUE

Thea

"Oh," I said slowly. "I should have thought of that."

"You and me both," Joe said dryly.

We were on a video call. He was working, as was I. I could hear the sound of an air-powered machine in the background.

"He wants you to come up next weekend, and I'm supposed to take you to the pizza place for a date. He promised to play in the play area." Joe's lips twitched with his smile.

I stared at the only man I'd ever loved, and my heart felt light as air followed by a piercing but sweet twist.

"That'd be nice," I whispered.

"It'd be more than nice," Joe said flatly.

"By the time you get here, it will have been three weeks since I last saw you."

I bit my lip, feeling the heat rise in my cheeks. "I know."

"It'll be worth the wait."

Our call was interrupted when Joe glanced over his shoulder. "Someone's knocking."

"Why are you staying open late today?" I asked.

He stood, carrying his phone with him to his office door. "I rotate having the garage open one late night a week. Dad always did that, and the locals love it. It's great for people who are too busy to drop their car off when they're at work."

"That's a great idea," I said, just as he opened the door.

Jack, one of the mechanics who worked for Joe and who I'd met when I'd been by the garage, waved at me. "Hey, Thea!"

"Hey, Jack," I offered with a return wave.

There was a pause as Joe conferred with Jack. When his face came back into view, I said, "I'll let you go. Sounds like you need to work."

"I do. Love you."

"Same."

We ended the call, and I leaned back in

my desk chair. I was still at my office. Some-times when I wanted to work late, I was more focused if I stayed here. I tapped a key on my keyboard, and my computer screen came to life. A click later, and I was staring at my calendar. It was Monday evening, and I had to wait all the way until Friday to see Joe. I didn't want to wait that long. I had vacation time that I would either have to cash out or use before I left.

———

It was a windy evening, but traffic was light. That was a major bonus to driving up from Boston during the week. During summer weekends in Maine on I-95 and Route 1, traffic could be bumper-to-bumper at times. Maine dubbed itself Vacationland for a rea-son. The flow of travelers from the East Coast was near constant on the weekends with some major cities close enough to make the drive worthwhile. On a Monday evening, the contrast was nice.

My dashboard lit up with an incoming call, and I smiled when I saw Joe's mother's name. I tapped the screen to answer on speaker.

"Hi, Maria."

"Hi, Thea. We're headed over to pick up Joey right now. You're in the clear," she said, her tone conspiratorial.

"You don't know how much I appreciate this," I said quickly.

I still felt a little nervous that I'd even had the nerve to call and ask her for help. She seemed to enjoy being a part of my plan, though.

"It is *never* a problem to babysit Joey. We're taking him to a movie. That way we can throw Joe off the scent as to why we called to take Joey tonight. You might want to check the garage first, or at least look for his car."

"I will. Thank you again."

There was a pause, just long enough that I prompted, "Maria?"

"Oh, I'm right here. I was just about to say I'm really glad you and Joe found each other again."

"Thank you. I'm feeling pretty lucky," I said honestly.

"Luck is only one part of love. Take it from someone who's been married for years and years. Soul mates are made. Don't forget that. You take care of my boy."

"I will."

Emotion welled inside, and I had to clear

my throat after that call. It meant more than Joe's mom could know that she said that. Although I knew intellectually it wasn't my fault, it still stung that my father had refused to allow me to keep dating Joe in high school. They were a tight family, and it meant a lot for her to be open to me.

A little while later, I smiled when I saw the exit announcing Haven's Bay in two miles. Butterflies took flight in my belly, and my pulse was racing. I wasn't even there yet, and I didn't need to be nervous. I'd never surprised Joe like this. I didn't even have to go out of my way to check on the garage. When I spied Joe's SUV in the employee area of the parking lot, I turned in. A few other vehicles were still there.

I sat in my car for a moment, gripping the steering wheel once I turned the engine off. I had already told Joe I loved him. I'd already said I'd marry him. But it felt as if these past few weeks had been a test I needed to pass.

Tonight wasn't the night, but I would eventually tell Joe those weekends apart had given me time to let the logic around my issues with fertility disentangle from the situation with Joey. Learning how Joey had connected dots that didn't actually connect about my presence in his dad's life and what was happening with his mother had clarified a lot for me. Just like children's minds could connect dots that didn't make sense, I'd done the same with my lingering grief about my infertility. I'd needed something to help me let that go, and I had.

I was still gripping the steering wheel when there was a light knock on my window. I shrieked, whipping my head to the side to see Joe standing there. He was in his mechanics outfit, which really did something for me. My belly flipped, and my pulse kicked off like a horse out of a gate, thundering forward.

I started to open the door, belatedly realizing my seat belt was still buckled. Joe chuckled as he finished opening the door for me. "This is a nice surprise. I'm filthy," he said, gesturing his hand up and down his body.

I let my eyes travel up and down his body, taking in the smears of grease on his overalls and just how delectable he looked. "I don't care."

Joy fizzed inside as I climbed out and stepped closer to him. All my emotions tangled together—joy, the piercing ache of missing him finally being relieved, letting go of my worries, and an intense, deep love.

He wrapped me in his arms, and I breathed in the scent of him. He smelled like the garage, but that scent was so closely entwined with him for me that it *was* him. Underneath it, I could smell that crisp, ocean scent that clung to him.

"You couldn't have known your timing was so good. Joey's with my parents tonight," he commented, the rumble of his voice rolling through me.

I leaned back to peer up at him. "It's possible I could have known." My lips stretched into a smile.

"Oh, you planned this. You called my parents? I didn't think much of it, but it was a little odd for them to plan a movie on Monday night." My smile widened. "God, I fucking love you," he murmured.

Then we were laughing together, and my giddiness at being with him spilled over. By the time we stopped laughing, we had tears in our eyes.

"Wow," I said when I could finally catch my breath. "I don't know why that was so funny."

Joe brushed my hair away from my face before pressing a lingering kiss on my lips. When he lifted his head, he said, "I have a few things to tie up inside. You want to come in and wait?"

I wasn't ready for this moment to pass. "In a minute." I placed my palm on his heart. I could feel the steady beat thumping against my palm. It anchored me in the maelstrom of my emotions. "I love you."

"I love you too," he said easily, just as easily as saying the sky was blue, or the grass was green.

Our love was a basic fact of the universe for us.

"Even though I missed you, I needed those weekends because I got a little—" I circled my hand beside my head in the air. "All up in my head about it when Joey thought I was trying to take his mom's place. I wasn't, but I also can't be a mom, not the way his mom is." Joe opened his mouth to say something, but I pressed my palm on his chest a little more firmly. "No, this is important. I know that the biological part of being a parent is just one part and that the *being* of it is more important, but my emotions needed to catch up with my brain."

Joe leaned down, his eyes holding mine like a magnetic force. "Good. We've got this."

"I know," I whispered.

"It's us. It's all we are. That's all that matters."

I bit my lip, and then we were kissing. I lost sense of everything but Joe until the sound of a car horn honking punctured my haze. We broke apart, gasping for air.

Jack rolled his eyes from where he stood beside a car nearby. "You're putting on a show, boss. Go in there and close up your office. I'll take care of that truck."

"You sure?" Joe asked.

"Yep."

Joe held my hand as we walked into the garage. He did close things up in his office, but not before kissing me indecently up against his office wall.

Thank you for reading Joe & Thea's story - I hope you loved it!

Want a glimpse of the future for Joe & Thea? Join my newsletter to receive an exclusive scene!

Sign up here: https://BookHip.com/ MQRLSVM

p.s. If you are already subscribed, you'll still be able to access the scene.

For more swoony romance...

This Crazy Love kicks off the Swoon Series - small town southern romance with enough heat to melt you! Jackson & Shay's story is epic - swoon-worthy & intensely emotional. Jackson just happens to be Shay's brother's best friend. He's also *seriously* easy on the eyes. Shay has a past, the kind of past she would most definitely like to forget. Past or not, Jackson is about to rock her world. Don't miss their story! Free on all retailers!

Burn For Me is a second chance romance for the ages. Sexy firefighters? Check. Rugged men? Check. Wrapped up together? Check. Brave the fire in this hot, small-town romance. Amelia & Cade were high school sweethearts & then it all fell apart. When they cross paths again, it's epic - don't miss Cade's story!
Free on all retailers!

For more small town romance, take a visit to

Last Frontier Lodge in Diamond Creek. A sexy, alpha SEAL meets his match with a brainy heroine in Take Me Home. Marley is all brains & Gage is all brawn. Sparks fly when their worlds collide. Don't miss Gage & Marley's story!
Free on all retailers!

If sports romance lights your spark, check out The Play. Liam is a British footballer who falls for Olivia, his doctor. A twist of forbidden heats up this swoon-worthy & laugh-out-loud romance. Don't miss Liam & Olivia's story.
Free on all retailers!

FIND MY BOOKS

Thank you for reading All We Are! I hope you enjoyed the story. If so, you can help other readers find my books in a variety of ways.

1) Write a review!
2) Sign up for my newsletter, so you can receive information about upcoming new releases & receive a FREE copy of one of my books: http://jhcroixauthor.com/subscribe/
3) Like and follow my Amazon Author page at https://amazon.com/author/jhcroix
4) Follow me on Bookbub at https://www.bookbub.com/authors/j-h-croix

5) Follow me on Instagram at https://www.instagram.com/jhcroix/

6) Like my Facebook page at https://www.facebook.com/jhcroix

———

Haven's Bay Holiday Series

All I Want - free on all retailers for the holiday season 2022!

All I Need - release date Nov 1, 2022

All We Have - release date Nov 15, 2022

All We Are - release date Nov 29, 2022

Light My Fire Series

Wild With You

Hold Me Now

Only Ever Us

Fall For Me

Keep Me Close

With Every Breath

All It Takes - coming Jan 2023!

Dare With Me Series

Crash Into You

Evers & Afters

Come To Me

Back To Us

Take Me There

After We Fall

Swoon Series

This Crazy Love
Wait For Me
Break My Fall
Truly Madly Mine
Still Go Crazy
If We Dare
Steal My Heart
Into The Fire Series
Burn For Me
Slow Burn
Burn So Bad
Hot Mess
Burn So Good
Sweet Fire
Play With Fire
Melt With You
Burn For You
Crash & Burn
That Snowy Night
Brit Boys Sports Romance
The Play
Big Win
Out Of Bounds
Play Me
Naughty Wish
Diamond Creek Alaska Novels
When Love Comes
Follow Love
Love Unbroken

Love Untamed
Tumble Into Love
Christmas Nights

Last Frontier Lodge Novels

Take Me Home
Love at Last
Just This Once
Falling Fast
Stay With Me
When We Fall
Hold Me Close
Crazy For You
Just Us

ACKNOWLEDGMENTS

The idea for Haven's Bay came about because I love the old houses on the coasts of Maine. One of our favorite things to do is drive along the coast here because it's stunning. Many of those homes are empty, some are falling apart, and others are neglected after families moved away. I thought it'd be the perfect setting for a holiday romance. It was only supposed to be one story.

But this is me! If you've read any of my stories, you know I love small towns and interconnected stories. I hope you loved this holiday visit to Haven's Bay, Maine. I'm planning to visit this town for more holiday stories, so you'll be able to return for more book vacations. ;)

So many thanks to my readers for reading my stories. I continue to be in awe and so grateful.

Much appreciation to my editor and to Terri D. for proofreading and making sure I keep my days of the week straight. My assistant is so patient with me and helps keep the details running smoothly.

I'm so thankful for my early readers who are the last line of defense for any stubborn errors. Although by the time a typo has survived four rounds of editing, maybe it deserves to stay.

As always, thanks to my husband and family for supporting my dreams and to my dogs for reminding me what unconditional love is.

xoxo

J.H. Croix

ABOUT THE AUTHOR

USA Today Bestselling Author J. H. Croix lives in a small town in Maine with her husband and two spoiled dogs. Croix writes swoony contemporary romance with sassy women and alpha men who aren't afraid to show some emotion. Her love for quirky small-towns and the characters that inhabit them shines through in her writing. When she's not writing, you can find her cooking, counting the turtles in her backyard pond, and running with her dogs, which is when her best plotting happens. Take a walk on the wild side of romance with her bestselling novels!

Places you can find me:
jhcroixauthor.com
jhcroix@jhcroix.com

facebook.com/jhcroix

instagram.com/jhcroix

bookbub.com/authors/j-h-croix

www.ingramcontent.com/pod-product-compliance
Lightning Source LLC
Chambersburg PA
CBHW061240210726
48293CB00003B/848